A Zen For Murder

Mooseamuck Island Cozy Mystery Series

Book 1

Leighann Dobbs

This is a work of fiction.

None of it is real. All names, places, and events are products of the author's imagination. Any resemblance to real names, places, or events are purely coincidental, and should not be construed as being real.

Chapter One

Claire Watkins tossed a dead rose stem from her spacious garden into the small wheelbarrow just as the sun made its appearance, splashing the blue Atlantic Ocean with a wash of pink.

Sunrise was her favorite time of day. It was quiet. Peaceful. To her, the hours before her little town of Crab Cove on Mooseamuck Island, Maine, woke up and the hubbub of tourist and local activity started were the most precious hours of the day.

Stretching, she winced at the slight pull in the muscles in her lower back and the popping sounds that crackled from her spine. Even so, Claire felt grateful that she enjoyed relatively good health for her seventy years, which she attributed to the strict natural health regimen she'd adopted in the past decade.

She'd never tire of looking at the panoramic view from her stone cottage, perched three-quarters of the way up Israel Head Hill on the small island off the coast of Maine. She'd grown up in this house and returned in later years to tend to her ailing father. Now, she lived here alone. Which suited her just fine.

Sucking in a deep breath of salty sea air, her gaze drifted from the ocean that stretched in front of her to the cove below, with its picturesque fishing boats on her left. Claire couldn't imagine living anywhere else.

She closed her eyes, letting her breath out slowly as she enjoyed the early morning island sounds.

The happy chirping of chickadees, wrens and nuthatches in her garden.

The familiar cry of gulls in the distance.

The soothing sound of the surf lapping at the shore.

The angry yelling and cursing coming from the road below.

Claire's eyes flew open.

Angry yelling and cursing?

That wasn't a normal, early morning sound on the island. She cocked her head, honing in on the direction of the noise. It sounded like it was coming from the scenic vista that overlooked the cove. She hurried to the patio in the corner of her yard that looked down on the vista.

Claire's father had installed the patio years ago in order to make the most use of the yard and its views. The property fell away drastically at the edge of the patio, so they'd put up a heavy-duty railing for safety. Claire could just barely see the road from her vantage point. She leaned precariously over the railing, the cliff falling away below her. Her brows rose when she saw who was causing the ruckus.

Norma Hopper, the island's resident artist, had setup her paint-splotched, wooden easel in her usual spot. For as long as Claire could remember, Norma had started the day at that very spot, where she painted the island sun-rises that she was famous for and which sold to tourists like hotcakes in the summer.

But today, her canvas was blank. Instead of painting, she was engaged in a heated argument with Zoila Rivers. The two women were squared off, facing each other, Norma with her hands on her hips, Zoila waving a piece of paper in Norma's face.

Snatches of angry words drifted up and, although Claire couldn't make out exactly what the words were, she could tell something serious was going on.

Norma stood rigid, the immense brim of her straw hat, which Claire had always suspected she wore more to keep people out of her space than to ward off the sun, stuck out like a quivering awning.

Zoila, in contrast, was a whirl of energy, shuffling her feet and waving her arms. Claire didn't know Zoila very well. The psychic had come to the island just over a year ago and, while some people didn't believe in her abilities, Claire had thought she was well-liked.

It wasn't unusual to see Norma acting angry. She was naturally abrasive, but everyone liked and respected her. Despite the artist's gruff demeanor, Claire had fond memories of Norma, who she'd known since she was a little girl growing up on the island. When Claire had returned a few years ago, she'd rekindled that friendship as an adult.

Claire knew Norma's usual, angry facade, though, and this wasn't it. Not only that, but Claire's training as a criminal psychologist made her an expert in body language ... and the body language of these two women told Claire this was no trifling matter.

As far as she knew, though, Zoila Rivers and Norma Hopper were only passing acquaintances. She couldn't imagine what could possibly cause them to argue so vehemently.

Claire pushed back from the railing and pulled her sweater tight around her to ward off the late spring chill that seemed to suddenly permeate the air. Then, she put her pruning shears away and rushed into the house. She'd better hurry and get ready for what the day may bring. Her intuition told her something unusual was afoot on Mooseamuck Island.

***

Further up Israel Head Hill, Dominic Benedetti sat on the patio of his condo, his great, bushy eyebrows drawn together in a disapproving 'V' as he regarded the cannoli on the plate in front of him. It wasn't the confection, so much, that drew his objection but the uneven placement of the tiny, chocolate-chip garnishments. Five on one side and six on the other.

Does no one take pride in their work anymore? he wondered as he picked it up and took a small bite.

The creamy pastry coated his tongue and he nodded. Almost as good as his Nonna made.

Almost, but not quite.

Nothing was quite as good as it had been in his youth, especially not the home-made Italian food he'd enjoyed or the culture of his close Italian neighborhood in the north end of Boston.

But then, one couldn't expect things to stay the same forever.

He sighed, his heart twisting as he looked past the French doors into the living room where the picture of Sophia, his late wife, sat in its sterling silver frame. They'd shared forty-five years and two children together, and though cancer had taken her from him almost two years ago, the loss still felt fresh and raw—like a big hole had been cut right out of him.

He wrenched his eyes from the picture and looked back down at the cannoli, his appetite fading as his memory rehashed those last few weeks with Sophia.

She'd made him promise to live a good long life. He'd agreed because it seemed to give her peace. But the truth was he didn't want to live a good long life—not without her. In the end, though, he'd tried to honor that wish. Which was why he'd come to Crab Cove—a place where they'd spent many happy vacations with their children. The kids were grown now and Sophia was gone, but Dom still loved the quaint New England island.

Living on the island had taken some of the sting from his loss and he had to admit he *had* started to enjoy himself a little. He'd even indulged himself in a few things Sophia wouldn't have approved of—like eating dessert for breakfast.

He sighed and bit into the cannoli again. When Sophia's death had dulled his zest for life, he'd retired from his investigative consulting practice to come up north and lick his wounds.

Adjusting to his new life hadn't been easy and he had to admit, now that time had dulled some of the pain, he was getting a little bored.

He listened to his parakeets, Romeo and Juliet, chirp away inside the condo while he finished off the pastry. He had been lonely at first, but the birds helped keep him company and the other residents of Crab Cove had made him feel right at home.

Dom allowed himself a thin smile as he mused about his newfound celebrity status on the island. Apparently, they didn't get many folks who had 'made the papers' up here, and Dom had made them plenty as a consulting detective on high profile cases down in Massachusetts.

But that was in his old life. Now, he had to amuse himself by finding runaway cats and lost sets of keys. Still, he did have a spectacular view from his condo, high atop the hill. One could have a much worse retirement.

He carefully wiped the crumbs from his lips and glanced to the east, over the vast Atlantic, to where the sun kissed the very edge of the ocean.

Time to start the day.

Dom was just about to rise out of his chair when a movement further down the hill caught his eye.

Claire Watkins.

It wasn't unusual that she'd be out in her garden at this time of day, but what she was doing out there *was* unusual. Quite unusual, indeed.

His eyes narrowed as he watched her lean over the railing. Clearly, she was straining to see something below. Dom wished her stone cottage was not blocking the view, because judging by the way she was positioning herself precariously over the railing, he could tell it must be something of the utmost interest.

Dom's eyebrows started to tingle with electricity—a feeling he recognized well and one he hadn't felt in a long time. For most of his adult life, his bushy eyebrows had been overly sensitive. He knew from experience that this sort of tingle meant something big was about to happen. As an investigator, they'd been a valuable asset—and to think his daughter had wanted him to trim them when he retired!

He watched with interest as Claire pushed off from the railing and hurried inside her cottage.

Then he, too, hurried inside, a spring in his step.

He carefully cleaned off his plate and dried it, putting it away on top of the stack of same-sized plates and patting the edges to make sure they were aligned perfectly. Romeo and Juliet twittered and peeped. He stopped in front of their cage on his way to the bedroom and the two birds became quiet.

Romeo fluffed up his green and yellow feathers and sidestepped along the perch toward Dom. Juliet remained in the corner, preening her white and aqua tail.

The birds' normal chattering was mostly gibberish, but every so often, Romeo surprised Dom by uttering an almost perceptible word in his high-pitched parakeet voice. Romeo looked sideways at Dom with one of his bright, black eyes and squalked, "Zoorious."

"Indeed, my little friend," Dom said as he clipped a millet spray to the side of the cage. "It certainly is *very* curious."

Chapter Two

Chowders Diner was a Crab Cove mainstay and a favorite of the locals. Tucked away on a side-street, it was not often found by tourists, which was fine with the island residents. It had the best food in town and they preferred to keep it to themselves.

The diner had been around since the 1930s. Originally run by prominent Mooseamuck Island resident Josiah Chase, it had been recently purchased by a newcomer—Sarah White. Claire had taken an immediate liking to Sarah, who she figured to be in her early thirties. Sarah was a pretty blonde, a bit too serious for her young age. Claire could tell that serious demeanor was caused by a dark secret.

Claire didn't know what the secret was, but she knew Sarah thought she was keeping it well-hidden. She was probably right, for the most part. If not for Claire's training, she wouldn't have suspected it, either. She'd tried to draw it out of Sarah on a few occasions, but it seemed Sarah wasn't ready. That was okay, Claire wanted to help, but she knew from experience that a person had to be ready before they could be helped.

Claire sat at the usual speckled Formica table by the window, where, on most mornings, her regular crowd gathered to start the day. These were the people she was most close to on the island—people she'd grown up with as a kid. They were more like family to her than mere neighbors ... well, most of them were.

The exception was Dominic Benedetti. Dom was a fairly new addition to their 'group' and Claire didn't know if she was happy about this. She'd known him in her previous life as a criminal psychologist in Boston, where they'd often been called in to consult on the same cases. Back then, they'd had a working relationship she could only describe as grudgingly respectful.

It wasn't that she didn't like Dom—he was a nice enough guy, on a personal level. But on a professional level, the two of them had gotten along like water and oil. Oh, sure, he was an excellent detective with uncanny skills of deduction, but their methods were so different that they often found themselves butting heads.

Claire had spent most of her life studying human behavior, so when called in on a case, that was what she used to solve it—the behavior of the people involved. Dom, on the other hand, insisted on using only facts. It had caused a lot of professional arguments between them, yet they'd always seemed to get their man in the end.

But that was a lifetime ago. They were both retired now, and Claire had vowed to forget about their professional disagreements and try to make friends with the man who now sat across the table from her.

Claire watched a swirl of steam curl up from her cup of red rooibos tea as she listened to the others at the table chat about island gossip. Claire's thoughts drifted to the argument she'd seen between Norma and Zoila just a few hours earlier and her chest tightened with anxiety.

Her eyes slid to the doorway. Where *was* Norma?

Usually, the ornery artist joined them here when she was done with her morning painting. Claire glanced at the clock over the counter—it was almost ten o'clock. Norma should be done painting by now, but if she wasn't here—

"What do you think, Claire?" Tom Landry's question pulled Claire from her thoughts and she looked up to see Dom scrutinizing her, which only heightened her anxiety.

She quickly looked away from Dom and addressed Tom. "Think of what?"

"I was saying how egg production on my free-range chickens is way up this spring," Tom said. "They say increased egg production is a prediction of good summer weather."

"Well, hopefully it doesn't mean your chickens are going to be running around my garden again," Mae Biddeford admonished him. "Last year, they nearly ruined my blueberry bushes and I need those berries for jam."

Tom tilted his head, narrowing his eyes at her. "My chickens provide good fertilizer for your berry bushes and you know it."

Mae huffed and Claire suppressed a smile. Tom Landry and Mae Biddeford were both past eighty. They'd grown up next door to each other and each now lived in the very family home they'd grown up in. Tom's was a small working farm with goats, chickens and a few cows. Mae's property boasted acres of fruit trees and bushes. The two of them had an ongoing feud, rumored to have started in kindergarten. They bickered constantly, but Claire suspected they secretly had the hots for each other. If only she could get *them* to realize it, too.

"Besides, it looks like you have plenty of berries." Tom pointed to a large bag sitting on the floor beside Mae's seat. "I assume that's filled with jam."

"Yes, I'm trading it to Florence Ryder for a permanent," Mae huffed.

Claire cringed and caught her best friend, Jane's, eye. The islanders often traded goods or services instead of paying money. It was an old tradition started by their grandparents and, since most of the regulars were from families that had been on the island for generations, they continued the tradition. But Mae went a little overboard with her jams and most everyone had more jam than they could possibly use. Claire and Jane had a running joke about it and Jane winked back at Claire in acknowledgment.

"I see Crabby Tours has opened up early this year," Jane said, changing the subject from jam to more seasonal matters.

"Probably trying to get a jump on Barnacle Bob's fleet this year," Alice James said, her knitting needles clacking together with a metallic beat as she stitched furiously. Alice was always knitting something ... most of which she traded as eagerly as Mae traded her jams.

"Seems like those two are opening earlier and earlier." Tom referred to the rivalry between the boat lines, who both ran whale watches, lobstering cruises and pleasure cruises in the summer.

They'd had a rivalry going on for decades and for the past several years, it seemed each had tried to get a jump on the other by opening for business first. Not that there was any shortage of customers for the cruises. Mooseamuck Island was a popular tourist destination, and soon the population of the island would quadruple. And a favorite tourist pastime was going on one or more of the cruises.

Jane sighed. "I suppose so, but that means tourist season is just around the corner and my job is going to get a lot busier."

As postmaster of the Island, Jane had it relatively easy from September to June, when it was just the locals. But handling mail for all the summer residents and tourists could be a lot of work. Jane usually had to hire temporary help.

"True. But it is good for the economy," Alice pointed out.

"Still, I just wish Crab Cove didn't get so crowded," Mae complained.

Claire's attention drifted over to the doorway as the others discussed the pros and cons of the upcoming wave of tourists. Still no sign of Norma.

"Waiting for someone?"

Claire jerked her attention back to the table to answer Dom's question. "What makes you ask that?"

Dom shrugged, his dark eyes looking at her curiously. "You keep looking at the door is all."

"Oh, no. My mind was just wandering." Claire's eyes narrowed at him. Just what was he getting at, anyway? He was staring at her expectantly, as if he knew something. And then it hit her—somehow, he must know about the fight she'd witnessed.

Claire remembered that he had a view of the cove from his condo at the top of the hill. Had he seen Norma and Zoila fighting? No, he couldn't have. She'd been on his patio before and knew he could only see as far as her garden from his place —her cottage blocked the scenic vista. And, since she could barely hear the two women, she was sure he couldn't have heard them, either.

He'd probably seen her straining over the railing, though. But why would that pique his interest? It wouldn't pique the interest of a normal person, but then Dominic Benedetti wasn't exactly what Claire would classify as a normal person. He was a born investigator with keenly honed instincts, and his instincts were probably kicking in right now.

Somehow, Claire knew it wouldn't do to have him digging into whatever was going on with Norma. Dom didn't *know* Norma like she did and he might misinterpret things. What those things were she didn't know, since she had no idea what was going on herself.

She couldn't help but glance at the door again. This time, much to her surprise, it flew open and ten-year-old Gordie Glenn skidded inside, his cheeks flushed with excitement.

The hubbub of noise ceased and everyone in the diner turned expectantly toward the door where Gordie stood, his eyes darting from one patron to the next.

"Gordie? What is it?" Alice prompted.

Gordie's eyes lighted on Alice. His mouth opened and then closed. Claire's heart filled with worry. Was something wrong with Gordie or one of the other kids? And then Gordy finally blurted it out.

"There's been a murder at the zen garden!"

Chapter Three

The zen garden was part of the meditation area in Mooseamuck Island's public gardens—a twenty-acre tract of conservation land with an ocean view. It was startling to hear about a murder in the most peaceful place on the island. There hadn't been a murder on Mooseamuck Island in over twenty years. Everyone in the diner was shocked ... and interested.

So, naturally, most of them headed on out to the garden to see for themselves. Some rode bicycles—a normal form of transportation on the island—and others carpooled.

Claire hitched a ride with Tom and sat quietly wedged in between him and Jane in the front of his pick-up truck.

Would it be Norma lying dead up there?

Gordy hadn't known who the victim was—he'd only heard about it on the ham radio. Robby Skinner, current chief of police and Claire's nephew, had called in to the mainland, requesting help. By Claire's estimation, it would take about thirty minutes before the mainland police could get their boat out, so they had some time before they would inevitably be shooed away from the crime scene.

They jumped out of Tom's truck and headed down the path where she could already see her nephew flapping his arms, trying to keep people away from the scene.

"Hey, Robby. What happened?" Dread clutched at Claire's heart as she craned her neck to peek over her nephew's shoulder.

"Murder is what happened." Robby's eyes reflected desperation and she felt a tug at her heart. She knew he'd never secured a murder scene before and she felt bad for him. But not bad enough to stop straining to see who it was lying in the sand. Her eyes raked over the body and relief washed over her.

Then concern.

The body wasn't Norma. It was Zoila.

Robby tried to block her view "You know you shouldn't be here."

Claire tore her eyes away from the body and looked at her nephew. He was a decent cop, but he *was* a small-town cop, which was perfect for their little island where most of the crime consisted of minor infractions. Even then, he sometimes consulted with her on cases and she figured she'd helped him solve a good number of them.

"Sorry, Robby. This is big news, though, and you can't keep the regulars away." She glanced behind her at the small crowd that had gathered.

It was mostly the regulars from the diner, but a few others had straggled in. "I figure it was better to come up and see if I could help out."

"Thanks." Robby's cheeks flushed and he kicked the dirt with the toes of his shiny, police-issue boots. "I had to call back to the mainland for the homicide crew. I'm not trained to investigate a homicide on my own. Until then, I gotta keep the scene secure."

"Of course. No one expects you to have that kind of expertise," Claire soothed. "I'll help keep the others back."

Her eyes drifted over his shoulder again and she took in the murder scene. The contrast of the still body lying in the peaceful circles of sand was startling. Not to mention the bloody mess that was Zoila's face. She'd been beaten, not shot or stabbed. But with what? Claire noticed the blood soaking into the sand beside the body, which was wearing the same outfit she'd been wearing during her fight with Norma.

And where was Norma?

Claire glanced around but didn't see her anywhere in the crowd.

"My word!" Mae gasped. "Who would do such a thing?"

Claire turned to see Mae's face had gone pale, her hand covering her mouth.

"That's a very good question." Dom raised a brow at Claire, as if she might know something.

Claire narrowed her eyes at Dom. "Yes, it is." She put her arm around Mae and walked her over to a bench out of view of the scene.

Why had he looked at her that way? She didn't know who would kill Zoila. Well, she had seen Zoila fighting with Norma, but Norma wasn't a killer. She wrinkled her brow, remembering the piece of paper Zoila had been waving in Norma's face … she didn't have that paper in her hand now.

Maybe she'd delivered the paper before her meditation. Or maybe the killer had taken it.

Claire watched Dom as he walked around slowly, just outside the confines of the yellow crime scene tape. At the edge of the zen garden, he squatted and tilted his head, studying the scene from a lower angle. He nodded, his lips pursed together in a thin line. Then he smoothed his eyebrows, stood and continued his walk to the other side of the garden.

Claire handed Mae over to Jane and wandered to where Dom and been. She squatted in the same spot. What had he found so interesting? The body lay crumpled, the legs at an impossible angle. The circles had been raked in the sand recently and were still almost perfect ... except for one smudged area.

A shoe print!

She looked closer. The print was distorted, but it looked large. Probably a man's shoe. One of the rocks was out of place, too, and—

A flurry of activity behind her broke her concentration and she turned to see the crowd parting, as if Moses was coming through.

Except it wasn't Moses. It was Detective Frank Zambuco, and he did not look pleased.

***

If there was one word Claire would use to describe Detective Frank Zambuco, it was overbearing. Or maybe annoying. Probably both. The man exuded an amount of energy unusual for his age, which Claire guessed to be about sixty— though it was hard to tell, given the ever-present scowl that normally contorted his face.

He whirled onto the scene, barking instructions, tapping his sausage-like fingers and whistling under his breath. His rumpled, blue, button-up shirt and stained, tan chinos were evidence he had no one at home to dress him. She was not surprised. She figured no woman would be able to put up with him for very long.

"Out of the way. Out of the way," Zambuco bellowed as he swatted his way toward Robby. "Don't you people know you are interfering with a crime scene?"

The crowd shrank back from him and he eyed them with beady, dark eyes. "Now, don't go too far any of you. You might all be suspects. At any rate, I'll want to question some of you." He turned to Claire. "Especially you."

"Me?"

"Yep, you seem to be the ringleader often enough."

"Well, I just came up with the others. I don't —"

"Right." Zambuco put his hand up to silence her and turned to Robby. "What have we got here?"

"Looks like she's been dead a few hours." Robby turned to look at the body. "It's Zoila Rivers."

"Rivers?" Zambuco's eyes narrowed. "Wasn't she some kind of fortune teller?"

"Psychic," Jane cut in.

Zambuco's left brow ticked up and he glanced at Jane. "Right. Psychic."

Zambuco walked over to the crime scene tape, lifted it and slipped under. He spent the next few minutes wandering around the scene, whistling to himself as he looked things over. His actions appeared to be aimless, but Claire knew they were anything but. Detective Zambuco might come off like a goof, but he was actually a very good detective. Which made her nervous because if Norma *was* somehow involved in this, he would find out.

Claire shook her head to clear her thoughts. *What was she thinking?* Of course, Norma had nothing to do with Zoila's death. She was sure once she talked to Norma, the argument would be explained and it wouldn't have anything to do with this.

Suddenly, Zambuco turned sharply toward the bystanders. "Which one of you found her?"

"I did." The tremulous voice came from the corner and Claire looked over to see thin, gray Sam Banes, head gardener, raising his hand tentatively.

"And what were you doing here?" Zambuco asked.

"I'm the gardener. I came to make sure the rakes were out. People are always taking them."

Zambuco looked around, presumably for the rakes. "And were they?"

"Oh ... I don't ..." Banes looked around. "I guess not. I forgot about them when I found Ms. Rivers."

"Ms. Rivers? You mean you knew her?"

"Of course. She comes here most mornings to meditate." Banes's face crumbled and he looked down at the ground. "Or *did,* I should say.

"And did you see anyone else this morning?"

"No, sir, but I was on the other end of the gardens, tending to the annuals. I just drove over in my truck." Banes pointed to the white and green Moosamuck Islands Public Works truck visible at the end of the path.

Zambuco nodded, then whirled around, his eyes scanning the small crowd. "And what about the rest of you? Did anyone see anything amiss up here?"

They shook their heads, almost as one.

"Okay. We need to get you people out of here and process this scene." Zambuco pointed at one of the detectives that he'd brought with him. "Smithfield, you get their names and numbers. Oh, and I want you to halt all boat traffic leaving the island, *including* the ferry."

"Whyever would you want to do that?" Mae asked.

Zambuco stopped what he was doing and glared at her, then stabbed his finger in the direction of the body.

"Judging by the coagulation of the blood, Ms. Rivers was murdered only a few hours ago. It's early in the season and I happen to know there's only three ferries a day right now. The first one doesn't arrive for another twenty minutes ... which means the killer is still somewhere on this island and I don't want him to get away."

Chapter Four

Dom went back to *Chowders* with the others, his mind mulling over what he'd observed at the crime scene. The method of murder had been brutal, which indicated there was an emotional element.

But why chose a public place like the zen garden?

It must have been the only opportunity that presented itself to the killer. Dom was certain the killer must have needed to silence Zoila right away—Zoila Rivers knew something and someone else didn't want her to talk.

Dom had observed the crime scene closely and noticed a few things that seemed strange. He had them catalogued in his photographic memory for future inspection. He'd also observed Claire's odd response to the body. She had seemed shocked, which would have been appropriate for a regular person, but with Claire's training and the number of crime scenes she'd attended, it was out of place. Dom was certain Claire had found something startling about the body—whether it was something on or around the body or the mere fact that it was Zoila, he didn't know.

Even now, Claire was acting strangely. He noticed her slight hesitation when Tom and Jane got out of the truck in the parking lot. Almost as if she was reluctant to join them in the diner.

"Surely, he can't stop us from leaving the island!" Alice said as she pulled a skein of light blue yarn out of her tote bag.

"Or the tourists from coming *to* the island," Tom added.

"That's right," Jane said. "I doubt the town council will allow that, and I think they have the final say."

"A killer on the island." Mae shivered and turned her wide, brown eyes to Dom. "Who do you think it is?"

"It must be a tourist. A stranger," Alice cut in, directing her words at Dom. "I mean, it couldn't be one of us islanders, could it?"

Dom preened his left eyebrow as he felt an ember of excitement start to glow in his chest. Just like the feeling he used to get when he was an active consultant. Before Sophia got sick and he retired. When life was exciting.

"It could be anybody," Dom replied. "Does anyone know if she had any enemies?"

They all looked at each other and shrugged.

"None that I know of," Tom said.

"Me, either." Jane added.

"Perhaps she became privy to sensitive information through her work," Dom suggested.

"She was a psychic, so she might have discovered information someone didn't want known."

Mae's brows shot up. "That's true. Maybe she had a vision about something bad that someone did."

Dom nodded wisely. "Yes, it could be. The police will probably want to check her latest clients. If she had sensitive information on someone, it stands to reason that person might be mad or upset. Can you think of anyone who has been acting strangely?"

Another round of shrugging occurred between everyone. Everyone except Claire, that is. Dom noticed that she kept glancing toward the door while she fidgeted in her chair.

Dom pressed his lips together. "It could be an old feud, too. But Zoila wasn't from the island, right?"

"Oh, no," Alice said to Dom. "She moved here about two years ago. Not long after you did. Bought old man Barrett's cabin up, near the conservation land."

"She said the old hunting camp had the perfect ambiance for her psychic readings," Jane added.

"And was she well-liked?" Dom asked.

Tom shrugged. "Well enough. She kind of kept to herself. Though I'm told plenty of townsfolk

33

snuck up to the camp for a reading or two, at times."

Dom smoothed his eyebrow. An old hunting camp? Secret meetings? This was getting better and better. But if Zoila lived in a remote camp, why wouldn't the killer just kill her there?

There was only one reason—the killer must have not had time to wait until Zoila went home to that cabin. Which probably meant something had happened earlier in the morning. Something unusual.

He stole a glance at Claire. Maybe even something that would cause Claire to lean over her railing for a better look.

He didn't have time to think about what that might be, though, because just then, the door opened and Detective Zambuco stormed in.

**

Zambuco's brows zoomed up when he spotted the crew at the table. He strode toward them, grabbing an empty chair and pulling it across the floor, then shoving it in between Dom and Jane before folding his tall frame into it.

Everyone at the table scooted their chairs around to make room.

"I'll have a root beer. Lots of ice," Zambuco said to Sarah, who had come over to take his order. Then he turned his sharp eyes to the rest of the people at the table. "So, what do you people think? Got any ideas who did it?"

"Us?" Jane's brows rose. "How would we know who did it?"

Zambuco tipped back in his chair and looked at Dom. "What about you, Benedetti? I know you've investigated quite a few crime scenes in your day. You must have an opinion."

Dom smiled patiently. "True. But I'm retired now."

Zambuco snapped his chair back to the ground, accepting the glass Sarah handed him.

"Let's hope you stay that way. I don't need you people meddling." Zambuco looked pointedly at Claire. "Especially you."

"Me?" Claire looked at him innocently.

"Yes," Zambuco said as he crunched an ice cube. "I know how you like to give your opinion even when it's not wanted."

Dom's lips curled up in a smile. He agreed with that. In fact, he had to stop himself from nodding so as not to hurt Claire's feelings.

Zambuco continued on. "Seeing as I have you all here, I'd like to get the ball rolling with some questions."

"Okay," Claire answered, and the others nodded their assent.

"Did any of you notice Ms. Rivers acting out of the ordinary this week?"

His question was met with silence. In fact, the entire diner was silent as the other patrons were carefully eavesdropping on the conversation. Dom figured that by now, word had spread about the murder, and everyone knew Zambuco was here to investigate it.

"So, no one noticed anything?" Zambuco persisted.

Everyone at the table shook their heads. The customers at other tables bent their heads together, whispering, probably asking each other the same question.

"Did she take on any new clients or have a falling out with any regular clients?"

Claire pressed her lips together. "I don't think any of us know much about her client list."

"Do any of you use her services?" Zambuco asked.

The diner was filled with more silence. The only sound was the clinking of ice cubes as Zambuco chugged down his root beer while everyone at the table looked each other over. Even though the people on Mooseamuck Island were like family, they still liked to keep their private

36

lives private. Dom wondered if anyone at the table *had* used Zoila's services and was afraid to mention it.

"Well, I certainly didn't," Mae said finally.

Tom shook his head. "Not me."

Alice's knitting needles clacked faster. "Nope."

Claire, Dom and Jane shook their heads.

Zambuco studied them with intelligent, bird-like eyes, then waved at Sarah and pointed to his glass for a refill. "Banes said Ms. Rivers meditated there every morning. Was that well-known?"

"Oh, yes, I would say so," Mae said. "Everyone knows everyone else's habits here on the island."

Sarah appeared at Zambuco's elbow and filled up his glass. He looked down into the glass thoughtfully, swirling the ice around. "So, then most anyone on the island could have done it. Even someone at this table."

Mae gasped. "Well, it certainly wasn't one of us!"

"No?" Zambuco chugged down the second root beer. "So, no one here had a beef with Ms. Rivers?"

"No." Claire spoke for all of them.

Zambuco tapped his fingers on the table. "And no one has anything to add?"

"No," they chorused.

Zambuco rose out of the chair and turned to address the rest of the diner patrons. "What about the rest of you? Does anyone know who might have wanted Zoila Rivers dead?"

Silence.

"Okay, then." He turned back to Dom's table. "I want you to all stay accessible. I might have more questions."

"Well, we can hardly go anywhere, since you've stopped the ferries," Mae huffed.

Zambuco screwed up his face. "I may not be able to get that to stick. But at least for now, we have everyone contained here on the island. If we figure out who the killer is, it will make it easier to catch him ... unless he's already fled on a private boat."

Don watched Zambuco march toward the door, practically knocking over Kenneth Barrett who was on his way in. Kenneth shrank back from the detective, who nodded a half-hearted acknowledgment before disappearing out into the parking lot, leaving the entire diner staring in his direction.

A blush of pink tinged Kenneth's neck as he noticed everyone still looking in his direction. "So, I guess you've all heard."

"Yep." Several people answered.

"It's scary thinking there's been a murder here." He said the word 'murder' gingerly, as if the very word coming off his tongue might mar his cleft-chinned, preppy good looks.

As Dom watched Kenneth make his way to the counter, the din of the diner slowly came up to its normal volume. Now, everyone was talking at once—asking the same questions.

Who could have killed Zoila?

And why?

Kenneth pushed a glass pie plate aside and leaned over the counter, directing his next words to Sarah. "I came over as soon as I heard. I hope this doesn't spook you too much. Our little island doesn't usually have any violent crime."

Dom noticed Sarah's lips curl in a smile, but the smile didn't reach her eyes. She was being polite, though Dom suspected Kenneth wanted more than a polite smile from the pretty diner owner.

"Oh, I'm fine." She waved her hand dismissively. "Where I come from murders happen all the time. Besides, from what I hear, it sounds like the killer had a reason to target Zoila. It's not like there's a maniac around randomly killing people."

"I should hope not!" Alice's knitting needles stopped in mid-purl.

"Yeah, I heard that, too. Anyway, I was wondering if you could send Ben down with an order later today," Kenneth said.

Sarah's face puckered into a frown. She glanced toward the back. "Ben's not in today."

"Oh?" Kenneth frowned.

"He took the day off."

Dom noticed Kenneth looked put-out. Like most wealthy people, he was used to getting what he wanted, when he wanted. But on Mooseamuck Island, options were limited. Especially those for take-out delivery.

Ben Campbell worked for Sarah doing dishes, light food prep, cleaning and delivering food that he carried in the basket of his bicycle. Dom smiled at the thought of Ben, and Sarah's kindness toward him. Ben was a grown man, but not mentally capable of holding a 'regular' job. Sarah had trusted him and taken the time to train him, and he had flourished with his new responsibilities which turned out to be incredibly important seeing as Ben's mother, Anna, who had cared for him his whole life now lay dying in the hospice center on the mainland.

Dom's stomach tightened as he thought of Anna. he hoped Ben hadn't taken the day off because his mother had taken a turn for the worse. But if she had, he knew the islanders

40

would rally around Ben and make sure he was taken care of. Most everyone on the island seemed to think of the sweet—natured young man as an extended member of their family.

Kenneth leaned sideways on the counter, so he could see both Sarah behind the counter and the others seated in the diner.

"I saw Zambuco leaving. Does he have any leads?" he asked, apparently not sharing any of Dom's concern about Ben's welfare.

"He didn't seem to," Jane answered.

"Sounded like he thought it might be a client," Mae added.

"Oh. A client," Kenneth nodded. "Right. Maybe someone got mad at one of her readings. She doesn't always see pleasant things."

"How do you know that?" Claire asked. "Did you use her services?"

"Who? Me? No." Kenneth waved his hands. "But I've heard from others. In fact, now that I think of it, she did seem upset yesterday when she called me out to the hunting camp."

"Why did she call you out to the camp?" Claire asked.

Kenneth shrugged. "She wanted to renovate it. She was asking me some questions about it yesterday. As you know, that camp had been in my family for generations and she wanted some history on how it had been added to over the years. Anyway, she seemed a little off, but I didn't really think much of it at the time."

"Off?" Claire looked at him with interest. "How so?"

"Anxious or upset, I guess."

"Did she say that anyone or anything in particular had upset her?" Dom cut in.

"No. Like I said, we didn't talk about that. So, I'm afraid I don't have any clues as to what would have upset her." Kenneth leaned back over the counter to address Sarah. "You be sure and call if you need anything."

"Thanks. I'll be fine," Sarah assured him.

Kenneth nodded, then pushed off and headed toward the door which opened, revealing Shane McDonough, fourth generation islander and local handyman.

"Hey, Shane might know something," Kenneth said as the two men passed each other. "Didn't I see you heading out toward Zoila Rivers' place yesterday?"

"What? Yeah, I was out there. Why?" He looked around the diner, obviously confused as to why everyone was looking back at him.

"She was murdered this morning," Mae blurted out.

"What?" Shane's handsome face scrunched up in surprise.

Dom watched Shane's reaction carefully. It seemed genuine enough, but then human nature was more Claire's department than his. Dom preferred to stick to hard, cold facts, and one fact was that Shane had seen Zoila yesterday. He stole a glance over at Claire and noticed that she, too, was studying Shane's reaction.

Shane walked to the counter. "Wow, that's crazy. Anyone know why she was killed?"

"Nope," Jane answered.

"What were you doing out there?" Claire asked.

"What?" Shane looked confused at her question, then his face cleared. "Oh, she asked me to give her an estimate on fixing that stone fireplace. Some of the mortar is loose and a few stones fell out. I can't imagine why anyone would kill her. Are they sure it was murder?"

"Absolutely," Dom said.

Shane leaned over the counter, concern on his face as he looked at Sarah. "You okay?"

Sara smiled at Shane. A genuine smile this time, Dom noticed.

"Yes, I'm fine." She produced a paper lunch bag from behind the counter and handed it to Shane. Shane reached for his wallet, but Sarah held up her hand to stop him. "Nope. It's on the house. Repayment for helping me fix the oven yesterday."

Dom smiled to himself. It seemed that all the eligible bachelors in town were falling over themselves with concern about Sarah. He could see why they would want to protect her. She had a vulnerable quality about her. But he could tell Sarah White was a woman who could take care of herself.

Dom himself had become very fond of her. Not as a suitor—those days were long gone for him and he was too old for Sarah. His interests were more of a fatherly nature. She was alone, with no family on the island, and so was he.

Which reminded him. At his insistence, Sarah was trying her hand at Italian pastry baking. She prided herself on her dessert selection and wanted to broaden her horizons. Dom had shared some of his Nonna's recipes with her. He wanted to help her out, but he also had a selfish motive—he normally had his pastry shipped from Boston's north end and it was getting rather expensive. Having a source that would help feed his Italian pastry addiction right on the island would be convenient and economical.

The first dish she was trying was one of Dom's favorites—ricotta pie—and she had promised to have a test pie ready for him today. With all the excitement, he'd forgotten.

Dom got up and went to the counter just as Shane was leaving with his paper bag.

Sarah turned her attention from Shane and flattered Dom with a smile—a real one that reached her sparkling, hazel eyes. "I bet you're expecting your pie, aren't you?"

"I've been holding my breath waiting for it," Dom teased. He stepped closer to the counter and felt something gritty under his feet. He looked down to see sand, which was odd, because Sarah kept the place spotless. That was one of the reasons he liked the diner so much. His gaze went to the door that Shane was just now closing. The carpenter must have tracked the sand in.

"Here it is." Sarah was holding up a vanilla-colored pie. The edges were perfectly golden brown and it looked dense and firm.

Dom took the pie from her. It was heavy, just as it should be. He lifted the plastic lid and delighted in the sweet vanilla scent that wafted out. "This smells *delizioso.*"

Sarah fixed him with a stern look. "Now, I'm expecting you to tell me the truth. No lying to spare my feelings. If it's good, I'll think about offering it to my customers."

"I will give it my full attention tonight and you will have my honest opinion tomorrow," Dom promised.

Another customer caught Sarah's attention and Dom turned back to the table.

"Well, I gotta take off," Claire said, just as Dom slid his pie onto the table. Then she stood, pulled a ten out of her pocket and slid it under her mug. "This should take care of my part plus a tip, but I'm sure you all will let me know if I owe anything."

Dom watched Claire hurry out of the diner.

"Well, she certainly rushed off abruptly," Mae said as she sipped her tea.

"Yeah. I guess she had somewhere to be," Tom added.

Dom glanced out the window in time to see Claire's little brown Fiat whip out onto the road. She did seem to be in a hurry, which made Dom wonder ... just where was Claire rushing off to?

Chapter Five

Claire had patiently waited for the right time to leave the diner, and finally she was on her way to the harbor. She had to talk to Norma, but she didn't want to just rush off and raise anyone's suspicions ... especially Dom. For some reason, she couldn't shake the feeling that he was watching her.

Detective Zambuco had clearly been looking for someone who had a problem with Zoila, and she wanted to get to Norma and find out what was going on between the two of them before Zambuco did. She just hoped she was the only one who had seen them fighting.

A pang of guilt stabbed at her as she pulled her car into the small parking lot in the quaint shopping area next to the Crab Cove harbor. She wasn't used to keeping information from people, and it had been difficult to keep quiet about the fight she'd seen between Norma and Zoila earlier that day—but her loyalty to Norma had won out. The woman had been almost like a mother to her when Claire's own mother had died when she was a teen, and she couldn't give up any information that might incriminate her. Especially since Claire knew Norma would never have killed anyone.

Claire felt certain Norma would have a good explanation—maybe even one that would help reveal the identity of the real killer.

Claire hurried past the shops, with their weathered clapboard siding. The cove, with its selection of stores, was a big tourist mecca and, even though it was still early in the season, there were quite a few tourists browsing. Claire paid them no mind as she breezed past the *Harbor Fudge Shoppe*, *Mim's Boutique*, and *Sandy's Beach Jewelry*.

She stopped in front of Norma's studio, *Hopper Gallery*, her stomach plummeting with disappointment—the lights were off and the studio was empty.

She stepped closer to the large, glass window, cupping her hand over her eyes to look inside. Norma's colorful paintings lined the walls, their gold frames adding a rich tone to the room. But Norma wasn't anywhere to be seen in the small space. Claire adjusted her position to look to the only other room in the studio—the bathroom—but the door was open and that, too, was empty.

Where could she be?

"If you're lookin' for Norma, she done took off in Bryan's boat a couple hours ago." The voice startled Claire, and she turned to see Jeremiah Woodward standing at her elbow.

48

"What?" Claire squinted at the old man.

"Yep, she commandeered Bryan's boat and sped out toward the mainland."

Claire's heart froze as she thought about Zambuco's warning—that the killer might flee in a boat.

"What was she going to the mainland for?" Claire asked.

"Didn't say."

"When was that?"

Jeremiah scrunched up his face and looked to the sky. "Well, the sun was over theyah'." He pointed to a spot left of where the sun was now. "So, I guess that was about eight or nine o'clock."

Claire looked at her watch. It was almost noon. They'd discovered the body about an hour ago, and Zambuco had said it was a few hours old. She wasn't sure how reliable Jeremiah's estimation of time was. The timeline was tight, but Norma taking off in the boat might actually prove her innocence if she wasn't on the island at the time of death. But then again, if the death happened before that, it could make her look guilty. Especially if she didn't come back.

"Whatcha all gawkin' at?" Norma's raspy voice came from behind and Claire's heart flooded with relief. Norma hadn't *fled* the island—she'd probably just gone for painting supplies or something. Even though the island had a small grocery store and hardware store, some things just couldn't be purchased there—including some of the paints and supplies Norma used for her artwork.

Claire turned to Norma and smiled, despite the older woman's grouchy demeanor. Norma looked from Claire to Jeremiah, her wide-brimmed hat casting a sinister shadow over her face, which was pulled down in an unpleasant scowl.

"Norma, I thought you were over at the mainland," Claire said.

"Oh, and *who* told you that?" Norma glared at Jeremiah.

"Sorry, I didn't know it was a secret," Jeremiah stuttered, wilting under her gaze. "It seemed like it was right important that you get there."

"Now, Jeremiah Woodward, you be minding your own business." Norma rapped her cane on the ground loudly and Jeremiah jumped. Then, she whirled on Claire. "And what do *you* want?'

Claire wasn't fazed by Norma's seemingly harsh treatment. She was used to the artist's gruff exterior and she didn't let that upset her, because she knew somewhere inside was a heart of gold. Sometimes you just had to look really hard for it.

"I came to talk to you." Claire slid her eyes over to Jeremiah, the movement negating the necessity for her to add the word 'alone'.

"Hrmphh. Well, be quick about it" Norma hung the cane on her arm. Its ivory bull-dog faced handle stared out at Claire through its red, garnet eyes while Norma fished for the key to her studio. "I have a commissioned painting I need to finish and don't have time for idle chit-chat."

"Ahh ... well ... I'll leave you ladies to it," Jeremiah backed away from them. Claire got the impression he was happy to be escaping.

Norma shoved the door open and gestured for Claire to precede her into the cramped studio—which Claire did, deftly avoiding the stacks of canvases that leaned against the walls as her nose adjusted to the smell of turpentine and oil paint.

"So, what do you want?" The old, wooden floor creaked as Norma walked the perimeter of the studio, looking at her paintings and ignoring Claire.

Claire was glad to see that Norma was acting normal—not at all like someone who had beaten another person to death just hours ago. But what else had she expected? She already knew Norma didn't do it.

Claire gave a mental head shake and looked up to see Norma assessing her with intelligent, dark eyes, the brows of which were slightly raised in question.

"You haven't heard about Zoila?"

Claire saw Norma flinch just slightly. Probably not enough that anyone else would have noticed, but Claire was trained to watch for those tell-tale flinches. The mention of Zoila's name had hit a nerve.

"What about her? No one should pay attention to what she has to say. The woman is mad." Norma stabbed her cane into the floor to accentuate the last word.

"Really? Why do you say that?"

Norma narrowed her eyes at Claire. She was too sharp to be tricked into giving anything away. "Why do you ask about her, anyway?"

"She was murdered this morning."

Norma's eyes widened. "Murdered? By whom?"

Claire noticed that Norma's reaction seemed to register genuine surprise. At what,exactly, Claire didn't know—the murder itself or the fact that Claire was asking. "They don't know who did it."

Norma let out a sigh and lowered herself onto the wooden chair behind the old metal desk, the only piece of furniture in the room.

She rested her cane against the side of the desk, then leaned her elbows on the surface, steepling her hands in front of her. Claire noticed her hands were dotted with red paint ... at least she hoped it was paint. She stepped closer to get a better look and noticed there was blue, white and brown dots, too. It wasn't unusual for Norma's hands to be dotted with paint—she was, after all, a painter.

"So, you came all the way here to tell me?" Norma asked.

"Well, yes." Claire didn't know what she had been expecting. Maybe she was hoping Norma would tell Claire how her and Zoila had fought about some benign matter that would obviously have nothing to do with her murder.

But she didn't. Instead, she said, "Why come all the way here? You thought finding out about it from someone else might be too much for a fragile old lady?"

"Well, no." Claire hesitated. Norma was anything but fragile. "I saw you fighting with Zoila this morning."

"And you think *I'm* the one who killed her?"

"No! Of course not. I just thought if you explained what it was about, then I could make sure Zambuco ruled you out as a suspect."

"Explain it to you?" Norma's eyebrows crept up to her hairline. "I don't think I need to explain myself to you. And what were you doing spying on me, anyway?"

"I wasn't spying. I could hardly avoid it. I could hear you from my garden."

"What were you doing up at the crack of dawn?"

"I always get up for sunrise. Anyway, if I heard you, someone else might have heard you, too, so it's best if you tell me what you were fighting about."

Norma's face hardened. "Well, if you heard us, then you must know what it was about."

"I only heard shouting. I couldn't make out what you were actually saying. Then I looked down and saw Zoila waving some kind of paper in your face. What was on that paper?"

"That's none of your business," Norma huffed.

"Look, I'm not trying to pry into your business," Claire reasoned. "Zambuco is looking for people to put on his suspect list—people who had an argument with Zoila. I'm just trying to get our ducks in a row, in case he starts looking in your direction."

Norma crossed her arms over her chest and stared at Claire. "Well, it was personal. I can't say what it was about."

54

Claire sighed. "So you can't tell me what you argued about or what was on that paper. Not even a hint."

"It's not for me to say what we talked about."

"Well, if you could just tell me the general subject—"

Norma shot out of her chair. "This is getting tiresome. I don't have to tell you what we talked about and I'm not going to."

"Yeah, I get that. But if you don't tell me, I can't help. And where did you run off to—"

"Enough!" Norma came out from behind the desk, took Claire's shoulders and turned her toward the door. "Now, I need you to leave. I have business to tend to."

Norma opened the door and pushed Claire out. Claire turned to face her friend. "But I'm only trying to help."

"I don't need any help. Now, shoo." Norma made shooing motions with her hand, shut the door in Claire's face and snapped the lock.

Claire stood on the steps, boiling over with anger, a seed of doubt sprouting in her gut.

What was the big secret Norma had with Zoila?

She stared through the glass window at Norma, who stood with her back to Claire, apparently inspecting a piece of art she had hanging on the back wall. Claire's fists clenched in frustration. She didn't know what the big deal was, but she knew Norma hadn't killed Zoila, and if her friend wouldn't help clear herself by telling Claire what the argument was about, then Claire had only one course of action.

She'd have to find the real killer before Norma ended up in jail for a crime she didn't commit.

Chapter Six

Dom laid down his fork with a satisfied sigh as he finished the last bite of a small sampling of Sarah's ricotta pie. It was creamy and sweet—just the way he liked it. He leaned back in his chair, remembering how his Nonna would sometimes add lemon or chocolate chips to the batter.

He closed his eyes, an excitement building inside him as he reflected on the morning's events. The fact that he wasn't on the police force or being called in as a consultant didn't dampen his enthusiasm. He felt more alive than he had in a long time—he had a real case to work on, and he knew exactly how to go about finding the killer.

Opening his eyes, he absently watched Romeo and Juliet twitter and preen in their cage while he mentally constructed a 'to-do' list. First off, he'd have to compile a list of suspects. But how would he do that without the authority of the police behind him? He couldn't very well commandeer Zoila's customer list to find out who she spoke to yesterday.

Romeo flew to the side of his cage to sharpen his beak on the cuttle-bone Dom had clipped inside. He peeked over the oval, chalk-like bone at Dom and let out a loud squawk.

"Squabin!"

"Good thinking." Dom nodded at the small bird. Zoila had talked to both Kenneth and Shane about renovating the cabin yesterday. Even though they weren't clients, Dom figured that was as good a place to start as any. Over the years, he'd learned to never leave any stone unturned. Even the most routine interview could reveal a vital clue.

A tap at his back door interrupted his thoughts, and he looked over to see Mae Biddeford, holding up a jar filled with something green.

Dear Lord, not another jar of jam. Dom glanced at his cupboard, already full to the brim with the jams that Mae forced on him almost every day. He pasted a smile on his face and opened the door.

"Hello. I thought I would bring you a jar of my famous zucchini relish." Mae shoved the jar toward him hopefully.

Not jam. Relish. As if he didn't have a dozen or so jars of those, too.

"Why, thank you." Dom took the jar, then upon noticing how Mae was hovering in the doorway, he opened the door and gestured to his kitchen. "Won't you come in?"

"Okay." Mae practically sprinted over the threshold. "I won't stay but a minute."

Dom hoped she would only stay a minute—he had lots to do.

He put the jar on the counter and turned to her expectantly. After a long career as an investigator, Dom knew when someone wanted to tell him something, and he could tell Mae Biddeford had something she was dying to get off her chest.

"It's been quite an exciting morning." Mae glanced sideways up at Dom, who nodded but didn't say anything while he waited patiently for her to get to the point.

Mae worried her bottom lip, then glanced at the back door. She leaned toward Dom conspiratorially, and in a low voice asked, "Will you be investigating it?"

Dom smoothed his eyebrow and pretended to think about it. "Do you think I should? Detective Zambuco is already on the case."

"Pshaw." Mae waved her hand. "What does he know? He's from the mainland. We need an islander here to do the case justice."

Dom was surprised at how proud he felt to be considered an 'islander', but he wondered if Mae was just buttering him up. He sensed she had something she wanted to tell him about the case, so he decided to give her the perfect opportunity. "Well, I wouldn't know where to start. I don't think Zambuco will share Zoila's client list with me."

"I may be able to help." Mae's eyes twinkled with excitement.

His bushy brows crept upwards. "Really?"

She nodded. "Yes. Well, I don't know if this means anything, but I happen to know that Velma and Hazel were seeing Zoila quite regularly. Their appointments were on Tuesdays."

"And yesterday was a Tuesday," Dom added. He pressed his lips together, picturing the elderly spinsters, Velma and Hazel, Who ran the *Gull View Inn*. They were sweet, gentle souls. "You don't think they had something to do with Zoila's death, do you?"

"Oh, no. But they might know something. Those two might seem dotty, but they don't miss a trick. And I know they were there yesterday because they stopped by Tom Landry's for eggs after and I overheard them talking from my garden." Mae looked at him sharply. "I wasn't eavesdropping or anything. I was tending to my raspberry bushes and their voices carried."

Dom chuckled to himself and turned toward the door. "Well, that certainly is helpful information. I will pay them a visit and see if they can shed any light on things."

Mae puffed up, satisfied she'd done her duty. "Glad to be of help. I'll just be on my way, then."

Dom opened the door and bid her goodbye. As he closed the door his excitement in the case turned to a pang of insecure doubt. What if he had lost his investigating skills? What if he was too old, or couldn't remember the right way to go about it?

It had been years since he'd investigated anything, and if he screwed up and his information sent the wrong person to jail, he'd never forgive himself.

Then again, if he didn't investigate and the wrong person went to jail because he wasn't there to give his input, he'd never forgive himself, either.

It was better that he investigate, Dom decided. He hurried to clean up the plate from his ricotta pie. He had four places to visit and he didn't have a minute to waste if he wanted to fit them all in today.

Chapter Seven

Even though the police were no longer there, the meditation garden still bore the mark of a violent crime. Yellow crime scene tape surrounded the area where the body had left an unmistakable impression in the sand.

Dom could see evidence that they had taken a cast of the lone footprint. Something about it bothered him. It looked out of place, marring the pattern of the concentric circles that had been traced in the sand.

It was hard to believe a violent murder had happened in such a peaceful place. Dom had never meditated the regular way, much less by the use of a zen garden, but he could see how immersing oneself in the repetitive motion of drawing patterns in the sand could be relaxing. Especially up here, where the air was filled with the fresh smell of the forest and the chirping of birds. It was a quiet place—a good place for reflection.

Dom doubted it had been this quiet earlier in the morning. The condition of the body told him that Zoila had struggled. Had she cried out? She must have ... but why had no one heard her?

"Can't go in they'ya."

Dom turned to see the gardener, Banes, standing beside the trash barrel, a scrunched up Coke can and an empty white bag in his hand. "I know. I was just looking."

Banes squinted at Dom. "Hey, ain't you that famous detective form Boston?"

Dom straightened with pride and preened his tingly left eyebrow.

"Well, I could hardly claim to be famous," he said modestly.

"Well, I heard about 'ya." Banes nodded toward the crime scene area. "I bet you got some ideas on who killed her."

"I'm afraid I don't. Not yet, anyway." Dom raised a brow at Banes. "What about you?"

"Me?" Banes took a step backward. "Why, I have no idea."

"And you didn't see anyone up here or hear anything this morning?" Dom ventured.

"No, sir. I was on the other side and I'm a little hard of hearing. I was actually a bit late on my rounds this morning. Had to clean up horse poop on the trail." Banes scrunched up his face. "Otherwise, I might have been here when ... well, you know."

Dom nodded. "So, just what are your tasks here?"

"Well, I usually come up and rake the garden." Banes pointed toward the sandy area. "I make sure there are no leaves or pine needles on the sand."

"Do you make these circles?" Dom indicated the intricate series of circles that radiated from the stones that seemed to be placed at random in the zen garden. It reminded him of the waves that radiated from a rock tossed into a pool of water.

"Yep. To start. The way it works is the people come and make their own circles with the rake. That's part of the meditation. But each morning, I come up and rake them out to start the day. It's kind of fun, really."

"And the rakes. Do you supply those?" Dom asked.

Banes sighed. "Yes. We have to keep a supply of them, because sometimes people walk off with them."

"And this morning, the rake was missing."

"Yep." Banes looked over at the crime scene and shuddered. "I guess it might have been the murder weapon."

"Could I see one of these rakes?"

"Sure, just let me throw this out." Banes indicated the trash he held in his hand. As Dom followed him to the trash can, he noticed the white bag was a take-out bag from *Chowders*.

"Do you get a lot of trash up here? You'd think the islanders would respect it more," Dom said.

"Didn't use 'ta, but it's happening more and more now." Banes tossed the trash in the can and shrugged. "Kids."

Dom frowned at the trash. He could see the crushed soda can being tossed out by reckless kids, but he wondered if kids would be bringing take-out bags from *Chowders* up here. He didn't think so.

He tore his attention from the trash and joined Banes at the small storage shed. The gardener unlocked the door and reached inside, producing a strange-looking wooden rake.

"There's a couple of different kinds of rakes for zen gardens, but this here's the kind of rake we use." Banes handed it over for Dom to inspect.

It wasn't too heavy and of simple construction. A handle with a metal piece at the end. One side of the metal was flat and the other had a series of short, sharp tines protruding from it.

"The flat end is used to smooth out the sand, and the end with the tines is used to make the swirls and patterns around the rocks in the garden," Banes added.

Dom fingered the tines thoughtfully. With enough force, they could have caused the injuries that had killed Zoila.

Had the killer used the zen garden rake for his murderous act? And, if so, what had he done with it afterwards?

***

The Barrett family had settled Mooseamuck Island back in the 1600s and had once owned most of the land. Over the years, parcels had been sold off, and even the old family hunting camp— the first structure on the island—had been sold by Kenneth to Zoila, less than two years ago.

The Barretts had kept the best piece of land for themselves, which included a mansion—the largest house on the island—situated on a point of land that was surrounded by the Atlantic Ocean on three sides.

Dom pulled his Smart Car around the circular drive and got out. A fountain splashed melodically in the middle of the driveway as Dom walked to the homes impressive, double-wide oak doors. He rang the bell.

After a few seconds, the door swung open and a man in a black jacket looked out at him.

"Yes?"

Dom stared back. *A butler, in this day and age? People still have them?*

"Hi," Dom said. "I'd like to see Kenneth Barrett, please."

"Master Kenneth is in the stables around back." The butler leaned out onto the step and pointed around the left side of the house, where Dom could see a fancy carriage house.

"Okay. Thanks." Dom turned and headed toward the stables, enjoying the view of rolling hills giving way to the cliffs and the Atlantic below. As he neared the carriage house, he heard a loud clatter and then cursing. Peeking his head in, he saw Kenneth in one of the stalls, standing amidst a messy pile of wooden-handled stall mucking tools.

"Ahem." Dom cleared his throat and Kenneth snapped his head up.

"Oh. Hi. I wasn't expecting anyone."

"You muck out the stalls yourself?" Dom asked incredulously. He couldn't picture Kenneth, who looked like a male model with his swoop of blond hair, blue eyes and Kirk Douglas chin doing this type of work.

Kenneth shrugged. "Sometimes. I find this type of work keeps me grounded."

Dom nodded, inhaling the earthy scent of leather, hay and horse manure. He noticed that even the stables had the air of the 'well-to-do'. The saddles and bridles neatly hung on the walls were of the finest quality. Even the barn implements piled in front of Kenneth had matching gold and maroon adornment on the handles—a color combination that was repeated in the rosettes on the bridles and the coat of arms that hung over the doorway.

"What can I do for you?" Kenneth worked his way out of the stall and motioned for Dom to follow him down the aisle. A palomino snickered as they passed her stall, her blonde mane swaying like corn silk as she bobbed her heard up and down. Kenneth stopped for a minute to stroke her velvety nose. Dom noticed the horses were in tip-top shape. This one was freshly groomed, her saddle shined and polished.

"In the diner, you mentioned that you talked to Zoila yesterday and she seemed agitated. I wanted to ask you more about that," Dom said.

Kenneth stopped and frowned at Dom. "Why? The police have already been here."

"Of course," Dom replied. "But I'm not with them."

"Oh, no? Then why are you asking?"

"Let's just say I want to make sure us islanders get a fair shake. Zambuco isn't from the island, so ..." Dom let his voice trail off, taking a moment to glance down at Kenneth's shoes. They were square toed—not a match to the footprint at the zen garden. Then again, this surely wasn't his only pair of shoes.

Kenneth stared at him for a few seconds, then Dom saw something change in his eyes. He nodded and spread his arms. "I don't know much. Like I said, Zoila lived in my family's old hunting camp. She was doing some minor renovations and found some pictures she wanted to give me. She also wanted to keep the history, so she asked me to come out and go over the various additions to the camp. She was interested in what year each room was added ... that sort of thing."

Dom gave an encouraging nod. "And ..."

"Well, that's it. I went out and showed her where the original camp was, then each section that had been added."

"You said she seemed agitated."

Kenneth's eyes darkened. "Oh, right. She did. She kept looking around, like she was expecting someone or something."

"Oh, really? And did anyone come?"

"No. It's pretty remote out there. The conservation land abuts three quarters of that lot." Kenneth's brows scrunched together. "Well, now that I think about it, someone rode by on a bicycle up the path that goes through the conservation land. She seemed really spooked about that."

"Who was it?"

"Just the Flannery kid. She relaxed once we saw who it was, but when we heard the bike coming, she seemed agitated." Kenneth hesitated, then added, "I just figured she was probably waiting for Ben to come back."

"Ben?"

"Yeah, Ben Campbell. The guy who works for Sarah. I saw him peddling away on his bike, like he was being chased by a demon on my way out there."

Dom's eyebrow twitched and he reached up to smooth it. "How interesting. Did she mention what he was doing there?"

"No. I assume he must have delivered some food up to her."

"Or he could have been a client."

"I suppose." Kenneth's face darkened. "Hey, you don't think—

Dom held up his hand, cutting him off. "Oh, no, I don't think. Not until I have all the facts, anyway. Right now, I've just begun to gather them."

"Okay, right. Wouldn't do to jump to conclusions."

"Nope. But you've been very helpful."

"Sure, anytime."

Dom turned to leave, walked a few steps, then pivoted around again. "Say, did you see anyone coming up to her place when you were leaving?"

Kenneth frowned. "Now that you mention it, yes, I did. I was driving away and passed Shane McDonough at the end of the road."

"And what time was that?"

Kenneth frowned. "Well, I'm not sure, but I wasn't there long. I guess it must have been about one o'clock."

"Okay. Thanks." Dom turned and left for good, this time, getting into his Smart Car and pulling around the fountain, then out of the driveway. As he pulled out onto the road, he saw Claire Watkins's brown Fiat taking a left into the driveway.

Dom waved and smiled, despite the feeling of irritation that swept through him. He was certain Claire was visiting Kenneth for the same reason he was. He was annoyed that Claire was investigating Zoila's murder. He didn't need her butting in with her touchy-feely methods.

Then again, joining forces with the woman might not be such a bad idea. Though she was annoying to work with, they had done good work in the past and her assistance had been vital in solving quite a few of the cases they'd been on together. Not only that, but he was convinced

Claire Watkins knew something and his instincts told him what she knew was a key piece on the puzzle of who murdered Zoila Rivers.

Chapter Eight

Claire eyed the silver Smart Car with irritation. She should have known Dom would be investigating. That was exactly what she didn't want. She was afraid he would misinterpret what was going on, with his 'stick to the facts' attitude. He was too rigid in his ways and Claire had a feeling this was a case where you had to consider the human aspect.

She knew the islanders better than Dom and would be able to interpret the clues more accurately with that knowledge. A feeling of dread settled on her as she parked next to the fountain. She just hoped she could find the killer before Dom or Zambuco went off half-cocked and arrested the wrong person.

Kenneth came round the side of the house as she was walking toward the front door. A scowl darkened his face when he saw her.

"I should have known you would show up," he said.

Claire frowned at him. Kenneth was in his mid-forties—a spoiled rich kid that Claire didn't have much use for. She'd never had much to do with him and judging by the rude comment he just slung at her, she'd been right not to.

"Why do you say that?"

"It's just that you seem to always wheedle your way into any criminal activity on the island. Sometimes, I wonder if your nephew actually solves any cases or if you do it for him."

Now she remembered. Kenneth and Robby had been rivals on the football team in high school. She'd have thought Kenneth would have forgotten about that by now. Claire chose to ignore his comments and get down to business.

"Have you been out riding?" she asked, indicating the horse dung on his boots.

"Earlier. I was just in the barn tidying up." He continued toward the house. "I know you're not here to make small talk. You're here to butt into the Zoila Rivers investigation."

"Well, I don't think *butt in* is the right phrase. I just want to make sure Zambuco doesn't arrest the wrong person."

She thought she saw Kenneth's face soften. "That's what Benedetti said, too."

"Yeah, I bet. So, what did you tell him?"

"Nothing, really. Because I don't know anything. I went over to talk about the cabin and she seemed agitated." He hesitated, then added, "Benedetti did seem rather interested when I told him Ben had been there."

74

Claire's brows mashed together. "Ben Campbell? You don't think Dom could suspect Ben?"

Kenneth shrugged. "He is a little odd."

"He's not mentally capable of murdering someone. He's almost like a child and one of the sweetest people I know." Claire's heart constricted thinking of the sweet, lovable Ben as a murder suspect. And what was even worse, Ben's mother Anna lay dying in hospice. He was all alone in the world, except for Norma who was Anna's best friend and cared for Ben like he was her own.

What if there was some odd piece of circumstantial evidence tying Ben to the murder, and Benedetti and Zambuco tried to pin it on him? Claire couldn't let that happen, even if it meant joining forces and 'playing nice' with Dominic Benedetti.

Kenneth was staring at her expectantly. "Is that all you wanted?"

"Did you see anyone else there?" Claire asked.

"Yep. Like I told Benedetti, Shane McDonough was pulling in as I pulled out."

"So, was Benedetti heading over to talk to Shane?"

Kenneth shrugged. "I guess so. Are you going to follow him over there?"

Claire didn't like his snooty tone, but she didn't bother to answer. She had already turned around and was heading for her car.

***

Luck smiled upon Dom as he drove through town on his way to the *Gull View Inn*. Shane's truck was parked at *Chowders,* offering a perfect opportunity to question Shane about his visit to Zoila, tell Sarah how much he enjoyed the ricotta pie and find out more about Ben.

It was mid-afternoon, so the diner was practically empty. Dom went straight to the counter. From his vantage point, he could see Shane fiddling with the large, stainless steel oven in the kitchen. The carpenter was on his knees, his feet out behind him. Dom took the opportunity to make note of his shoes. They had a round toe, like the footprint, but he noticed something distinctive about them—the tread was almost all worn off.

Had the footprint in the zen garden shown no treads?

Dom couldn't remember whether it did or not, and he had a momentary pang of uncertainty about his detecting skills. Back in the day, he would have had all that information catalogued in his sharp memory. Then again, he'd also had the advantage of being able to look at the police reports to refresh that memory whenever he wanted.

He caught Sarah's eye. She smiled, and came to stand on the opposite side of the counter. "Hey, Dom. Did you try the pie?"

"It was *delizioso!*" Dom pressed the tips of his fingers to his lips and then spread them apart in the air.

"So, you think I should start serving it here?"

"I sure would buy them if you did. In fact, I wouldn't mind ordering one special right now."

"I'll get right on that." Sarah grabbed the napkin-wrapped silverware from under the counter and placed it in front of Dom. "What can I get you?"

"Well, actually I came to talk to Shane."

Sarah's brows ticked up and Shane looked back over his shoulder from his position in front of the oven. "Me?"

"Yes. I just have a few questions about Zoila."

"Oh, are you investigating the murder?" Shane pushed himself up from the floor and wiped his hands on a kitchen towel as he walked over to the counter.

Dom shook his head. "Not officially, but I figured I could look into it in case Zambuco comes to the wrong conclusion."

"Oh, well, that's probably a good idea," Shane said. "I don't really see how I can help you, though."

"Earlier this morning, you said you'd been out at her place yesterday."

Shane narrowed his eyes. "That's true. Like I said, she wanted an estimate on the chimney and some of the renovations on the camp."

"And what did the renovations entail?"

"She wanted the kitchen modernized and that old fieldstone fireplace repaired. There were some loose rocks in it." Shane's voice took on an edge of agitation. "What's that got to do with her getting murdered?"

"Probably nothing," Dom soothed. "I'm just trying to be thorough."

Shane ran his hands through his thick, dark hair. "Oh, well, I don't see how this can help."

Dom smiled. "I'm just trying to get an idea of what was going on on her last day. Did she seem upset at all?"

Shane's eyes slid to the left, his brow creasing. "Upset? What do you mean?"

"Did she act angry or on edge?"

"No. She seemed fine to me."

Dom pressed his lips together. "Kenneth said he saw her right before you and she seemed anxious."

Shane looked at Dom strangely. "Kenneth Barrett?"

Dom nodded. "He was there right before you. Said he passed you on the way out, actually."

"Oh, that's right. I do remember seeing him drive by. I didn't realize he was coming from Zoila's."

"What time were you there?" Dom asked.

Shane looked down at the floor, then back up at Dom. "I'd say it was around three thirty or four o'clock."

"Are you sure?"

"Yep. I don't watch the clock or anything, but I headed over when I was done at the Kirkpatricks', and that had to be after three."

Dom frowned. He could have sworn Kenneth said he'd seen Shane earlier. "And you were at the Kirkpatricks' this morning?"

Shane's eyes got even narrower. "No. And I don't like what you are insinuating."

Dom shrugged. "I'm not trying to insinuate anything, just trying to figure out where everyone was this morning. So, where were you?"

Shane's neck reddened, but he held his temper. "If you must know, I was at the Durants', repointing the brick on their chimney."

Dom noticed Sarah intently watching the conversation, her eyes pivoting nervously back and forth between Shane and Dom. He turned his attention to her.

"And what about Ben?"

Sarah's eyes widened.

"What about him?" Her voice rose defensively.

"Did he deliver sandwiches to Zoila?"

"Zoila? No, she never ordered from here."

Dom's brows shot up. "Really? But Kenneth saw him peddling away from Zoila's yesterday. Did he know her?"

Sarah and Shane exchanged a glance. "I don't think so. I mean, not any more than anyone else on the island."

"And Ben does do deliveryies for you, right?"

"Yes, he delivers between eleven thirty and one thirty every day, after he finishes his morning tasks in the kitchen. I could hardly run the place without him, now." Sarah's voice rose proudly, like a teacher praising the accomplishments of a favorite student.

"Where is Ben now? Doesn't he usually work today?"

Sarah crossed her arms over her chest. "Yes, but he called in sick."

"Oh, really? Does he do that a lot?"

"No, but when you're sick, you're sick." Sarah glared at him, and Dom wondered if he'd be getting that ricotta pie after all. "I hope you're not implying that Ben had something to do with this. He couldn't. He doesn't have a mean bone in his body."

"Oh, no," Dom held is hand up. "I don't have any suspects, yet. I'm just trying to get the timeline straight."

"Well, that's good." Sarah relaxed. "And besides, Ben couldn't have done it."

"Why not?"

"He visits his mother every Monday, Wednesday and Friday morning. I don't even think he was on the island when Zoila was murdered."

Dom's eyebrows tingled. There were quite a few inconsistencies starting to appear in this case, between what he'd heard from Sarah, Shane and Kenneth. Someone wasn't being totally honest, but the question was … which one of them was lying, and why?

Chapter Nine

The *Gull View Inn* was the quintessential Maine bed and breakfast. A sprawling, white Victorian with green shutters, it had a white trellised archway covered in lush rose vines that led to the generous, white wrap-around porch, also covered in rose vines. It was too early in the season for blooms, but the porch was alive in green leaves.

Dom sat in one of the white, wicker rockers on that very porch, being catered to by Velma and Hazel, the two spinsters who ran the Inn.

It was almost pleasant. Not like the interviews he'd conducted when he was on the job, Dom thought, as he gazed out over the vast waters of the Atlantic, watching the sun dance on top of the waves. The gulls cried in the distance and ice cubes clinked in his lemonade glass as he rocked lazily.

"I still can't believe it." Velma's white bun bobbed as she shook her head. "A murder, right here on the island."

"I know," Hazel replied. "It's disturbing."

Dom studied the two women, thinking they looked more excited than disturbed.

"You don't think we are in danger, do you?" Velma asked.

"Oh, no," he assured them. "We'll find who did it soon enough. In fact, you might be able to help."

"Us?" Hazel wrinlked her brow, her green eyes sparkling. "Oh, I don't see how."

"I heard the two of you had seen Zoila for a reading yesterday," he ventured.

Hazel looked at Velma who nodded. "Yes, we did. We saw her regularly."

"Did she say anything unusual, or seem out of sorts when you saw her yesterday?"

Hazel shrugged. "No, I don't think so."

"What did you talk about?"

Velma held a plate of iced gingersnaps in front of Dom, who eagerly accepted. "Well, I hope you don't think we're odd, but we talk to my daddy through her ... you know, about running the inn."

"You do?" Dom knew the inn had been in Velma's family for generations and that she'd inherited it when her father passed away decades ago.

"Yes, he still gives me great advice."

"You didn't see anything out of the ordinary when you were there?"

The two women looked at each other and shrugged. "Nope."

"Did she act any different than other times you'd been there, or seem agitated or nervous?"

84

"She did have a hard time channeling Daddy. She said her energy wasn't in tune or something," Velma said. "But honestly, I don't think she was a very good psychic."

"Why not?" Dom asked

"Well, if she was, you'd think she would have been able to see her own death and takes steps to avoid it from happening."

Hazel pressed her lips together. "I don't think it quite works like that, Vel. Remember how she said only certain things were revealed, and sometimes she didn't know exactly what they meant."

"Oh, right, like the time she thought Daddy was telling us to serve fruitcake at Christmas," Velma said.

Hazel chuckled. "Yes! But he really meant that your cousin Chris was a fruitcake!"

Velma nodded. "We had twenty fruitcakes we had to get rid of that year."

They all laughed, and then Velma's laughter stopped abruptly as her eyes moved to something just beyond Dom's shoulder.

Dom turned around, his stomach sinking when he saw Zambuco standing behind him.

"Well, isn't this nice." Zambuco nodded at Velma and Hazel, then narrowed his eyes at Dom.

Dom smiled. "Detective Zambuco, it's so nice to see you. What brings you here?"

Zambuco plopped down, uninvited, in a rocker. "Probably the same thing that brought you here."

"Me? I was just drinking lemonade and chatting with Velma and Hazel."

"Uh-huh." Zambuco eyed the three of them suspiciously.

"Ginger snap?" Velma handed the plate to Zambuco.

"Don't mind if I do." Zambuco grabbed a cookie from the plate with his giant hands and bit into it, crumbs falling on his shirt, and Dom guessed he either didn't notice or didn't care since he made no move to wipe them away.

"Now, Hazel, where are our manners. Let's get the detective a lemonade," Velma twittered.

"Lots of ice, please," Zambuco called after Velma, who had immediately sprinted for the front door.

The three of them were silent while they waited for Velma. Dom listened to the seagulls while Zambuco's thick fingers tapped a rhythm on the arm of his chair.

Velma returned with the drink. Zambuco looked at it and nodded.

"Thanks," he said, then chugged down most of it.

"Now, what can we do for you, Detective?" Hazel's keen eyes watched Zambuco as he bit into another cookie.

"Well, if you haven't given all the good information to Benedetti, I'd like to know what you can tell me about Zoila Rivers."

"Oh, we don't know much. Like we told Dom, we go there every Tuesday to talk to Velma's daddy about business matters."

"Velma's daddy?" Zambuco scrunched his face up. "He's still alive? And what was he doing at Zoila's?"

Velma laughed and swatted at Zambuco's arm. "No, silly, she channeled him. We talked to his spirit."

"Oh." Zambuco gave Dom a sideways look and rolled his eyes, as if he was wondering if the two elderly women were nuts and whether or not he should trust any information he got from them.

Dom simply shrugged.

"And what was her demeanor?" Zambuco continued.

"She seemed fine. Same as always," Hazel said.

"Well, she did have a hard time channeling, like we were telling Dom," Velma added.

Hazel nodded. "Thats right. Said her energy was a little off."

"But then, Daddy came through and told us to think about running a clambake on the first Sunday of the month." Velma turned to Dom. "What do you think about that?"

"That sounds like a fine idea." Dom took a sip of his lemonade. He was down to the bottom of the glass—the best part, where all the sugar was.

"We could serve steamers and corn, and—"

"Ahem." Zambuco cut Hazel off. "Did she mention anything in particular that was bothering her?"

Velma and Hazel both shook their heads. "Nope."

"She didn't mention having a disagreement or argument with anyone?"

Velma's forehead creased. "She didn't mention anything yesterday when we saw her ... but she *did* have a fight with someone this morning."

"She did?" Both Dom and Zambuco leaned forward, their attention focused on Velma.

"Velma!" Hazel said sharply.

Velma looked stricken. "Oh, dear ... I guess I shouldn't have blurted that out."

"Who did she have the fight with?" Zambuco asked.

Velma chewed her bottom lip, her eyes going from Hazel to Dom to Zambuco. "I can't say. I mean, I wouldn't want you to get the wrong idea about the person she fought with."

"Well, now you *have* to tell me," Zambuco said. "Otherwise, it would be considered withholding information and there might be dire consequences."

Velma's eyes widened. "You mean I could go to jail?"

"You won't have to go to jail," a voice cut in from the porch steps and Dom turned to see Claire Watkins. "And Zambuco won't force you to rat out your neighbor, either."

"I won't?" Velma's shoulders relaxed with relief.

Claire walked over to them and stood in front of Zambuco, her hands fisted on her hips. "No, Velma, you won't have to because I saw the fight, too. And I'm sure someone else did as well, so eventually, Zambuco will find out who Zoila argued with."

"For crying out loud, someone just tell me who it was before I throw the lot of you in jail!" Zambuco said.

Claire paused, then sighed. "Fine. I'm sure you'll find out soon enough. The person Zoila had an argument with was Norma Hopper."

Chapter Ten

Zambuco squinted up at Claire. "Norma Hopper? That mean old painter lady?"

Claire's gut twisted. She hadn't wanted to tell Zambuco it was Norma, but she couldn't stand him threatening Velma. She didn't want poor Velma to have to bear the burden of being the one who told him, so Claire had blurted it out. Anyway, he'd probably find out from someone else and this way, she could watch his reaction and try to temper the news.

"She's not mean," Claire said defensively.

"That's true," Hazel added. "She just acts that way. Once you get to know her, you realize she's not that bad."

Velma nodded. "That's right. We've known her our whole lives. She's crotchety, but she's not a killer."

"What did she and Zoila argue about?"

"I don't know." Velma pointed to her ear. "My hearing isn't as good as it used to be."

"Me, either. I could just tell they were yelling." Hazel looked up at Claire. "Do you know what they were arguing about?"

Claire shook her head. "No, I saw them from my garden. I could hear voices but couldn't make out the words."

Zambuco narrowed his eyes. "You ladies wouldn't be withholding information from me, would you? Because I'm pretty sure you had the opportunity to tell me this before Watson."

Clair grimaced. "I didn't think it was relevant, because Norma isn't the killer."

"Really?" Zambuco glared at her with sharp, dark eyes. "And what else haven't you told me because you don't think it's *relevant*?"

Claire held up her hands. "Nothing, I swear."

Except the fact that Norma left the island early this morning.

"Well, it looks like I'll be paying a visit to Norma Hopper." Zambuco pushed up from the chair.

"You're wasting your time," Claire said.

"Maybe."

"Do you have any clues that even point to her?" Claire asked, seeing the perfect opportunity to try and find out what clues the close-mouthed detective actually did have.

Zambuco picked his glass up from the small table beside his chair, tipped it to his lips and took in a mouthful of ice cubes, which he crunched noisily. "We have the footprint down at the lab. Of course, we are still missing the murder weapon, which I'm hoping will be found on the killer's premises."

"The rake?" Dom asked.

"Maybe. Anyway, the last thing you people need is to know what the clues are." Zambuco pointed his index finger accusingly at Dom and then Claire. "I know the two of you can't help but stick your noses in, but remember, you're both *retired* now. I wouldn't want to have to arrest you on obstruction charges and don't even think about withholding pertinent information again or you may find yourself in the cell next to your friend."

Zambuco slid one last warning look at Claire and Dom, bowed to Velma and Hazel and then stormed off the porch.

***

"Oh, dear, I hope I didn't get Norma in trouble." Velma's hands fluttered nervously in her lap. "I didn't even think ... I mean, he asked and I just answered."

"It's okay," Claire soothed. "He was bound to find out sooner or later, and better he hear it from us than someone who might not like Norma as much."

"But now I wonder ..." Hazel's voice trailed off as she watched Zambuco's car speed off. "You know how obstinate Norma can be. I hope she doesn't do something stupid and get herself arrested."

"That's exactly what I was thinking," Claire said. "That's why we need to figure out who did this before Zambuco jumps to any conclusions. That's why I came here, actually—to see what you knew."

"We don't know anything, really," Hazel said. "We were just telling Dom that our weekly visit with Zoila was uneventful."

Velma looked regretful. "Unfortunately, we don't have any clues as to who killed her."

Claire turned to Dom. "So you *are* looking into this."

He nodded slightly. "And apparently, you are as well."

"Yeah, kind of like old times." *Old times she'd rather not relive.*

"Almost," Dom said. "Except this time, we don't *have* to work together."

It was true. When they were on the job as paid consultants, they didn't have a choice. But now, they didn't have to join forces. Although Claire knew they would get the job done faster—and probably better—together. It was just so *annoying* to have to put up with Dom's insistence on only considering hard, cold facts when she knew her assessment of the human factor was accurate.

94

Claire sighed and plopped down into the chair Zambuco had just vacated. She might regret this, but she could really use Dom's help. If Norma was going to be as tight-lipped with Zambuco as she had been with Claire, he might misunderstand and take that to mean she was guilty. Teaming up with Dom offered the best chance to find the killer fast ... before Zambuco could gather evidence against Norma.

"But we could work together if we wanted." Claire looked at Dom out of the corner of her eye.

"We could," Dom said cautiously. "But as I recall, you used to get very irritated with me."

"And you with me." Claire bit into a ginger-snap, swirling the spicy-sweet taste around in her mouth. "But maybe for the good of finding the murderer, we could try to work together again."

"Well, we did catch quite a few bad guys back in the day," Dom said proudly, over the rim of his lemonade glass

Claire noticed a familiar flicker in his eyes—a spark of light from deep within. The same spark she used to see when they were on a case. Back then, his eyes would light up with excitement. She remembered how that light had been extinguished when his wife got sick. Now, it was back and Claire felt her heart soar for him. She realized this case was about much more than just finding a murderer for him ... and maybe it was for her, too.

"So what do you say? Can we work together?" Claire stuck her hand out.

Dom regarded her hand cautiously, then nodded and extended his own for a firm shake. "Yes, I think we can."

Velma and Hattie, who had been following the conversation, silently picked up their lemonade glasses and held them out so the four could clink rims.

"Here's to the two of you finding the killer so we can all sleep at night!" Hazel said.

"Here! Here!" Velma added.

Claire's stomach twisted as she clinked glasses with the others. Would she and Dom be able to work together to convince Zambuco Norma wasn't the killer and set him on the path toward the real murderer? Claire sure hoped so, because from where she was sitting, if she didn't know Norma the way she did, she'd be putting her at the top of the suspect list, just like Zambuco was probably doing right now.

Chapter Eleven

Dom loved sitting at the docks down in Crab Cove and watching the boats glide in and out of the small harbor. Right now, however, his attention was on Claire, who sat beside him recounting how she had witnessed the fight between Norma and Zoila that morning.

"So that's why you were leaning over your railing like that?" Dom snapped a pistachio out of its shell and popped it into his mouth.

Claire's brow creased. "You saw me?"

"Yes, I was on my patio. Could hardly miss you leaning over like that. I wasn't sure if you would fall down the hillside or not.

Claire laughed. "Well, I have to say I *was* glad Daddy spent the extra money to have those railings cemented in."

"So, what were they fighting about?"

Claire's face darkened. "That's the thing. I couldn't hear what they were saying, just that they were yelling. Zoila had a paper in her hands and she was waving it in front of Norma."

Dom's eyebrows tingled. "A paper? What kind of paper?"

Claire scrunched up her face. "I'm not sure. I mean, they were pretty far away."

"Was it writing paper? Or newspaper? How many pieces?"

Claire closed her eyes and tried to remember. For once, she wished she had Dom's eye for detail. "I think it was one piece. It looked old."

"Hmmm. She didn't have any piece of paper when she was killed. At least, I didn't see one at the scene." Dom leaned back in the chair and looked out at the cove. From where he sat, he could see the row of shops to the left. Mae Biddeford was walking down the sidewalk purposefully. He watched her go into the seafood store with three jars of purple jam clutched in her hand—grape, Dom assumed. He popped two more pistachios into his mouth. "Any idea what was on it?"

Claire shook her head.

Dom stared out at the cove. He was beginning to regret his decision to team up with Claire—so far, she hadn't produced much valuable information. But there was still time. "Did you ask Norma about it?"

"Yes. She practically threw me out of her studio. Didn't want to talk about it."

Dom munched his pistachio thoughtfully. "So, after the fight, Norma went right to her studio? Did anyone see her?"

"Well, she didn't actually go *right* to her studio ..."

Dom turned sharply to Claire. "Where did she go?"

Claire sighed and looked out over the cove. "She took one of the boats."

Dom's brows shot up. *Now they were getting somewhere.* "She left the island?"

"Yep."

"Where did she go in the boat?"

"She wouldn't tell me."

Dom picked another pistachio out of the thin, pink and white striped bag as he thought about the murder weapon. Could Norma have taken it out to sea to dispose of it? If she had, someone would have seen her with it. "Did anyone see her leave the island?"

"Yes, she borrowed Bryan's boat and Jeremiah Woodward saw her."

"Did they see if she had the zen garden rake with her?"

"The rake? Why would she have that?"

"We think it was the murder weapon."

Claire's back stiffened. "Oh, so you think she was disposing of it. Well, I can assure you she wasn't doing that, because she isn't the killer."

Dom settled back on the bench. He remembered that in the cases they'd worked together in the past, he could always count on Claire's assessment of the suspects as being spot on. He respected her opinion in that area, but he wondered if her judgment was clouded by her friendship with Norma.

"How can you be so sure that Norma didn't kill Zoila?" Dom asked.

"I *know* her. She's not the type. Plus, she seemed shocked when I told her how I'd seen them fighting and that Zoila had been murdered hours later."

Shocked about the murder, or shocked Claire had witnessed the fight? Dom wondered.

"We can't go on emotion. We must go with the facts and solid clues. Of which we have very few," Dom said. "We need to find out what the police know about this footprint."

Claire chewed her bottom lip. "Maybe I could get my nephew to tell us. He owes me for all the cases I've helped him with."

"And we should try to reconstruct Zoila's morning, and probably the prior day."

Claire smiled. "Just like old times."

"Exactly. Except we don't have the benefit of the police badge and associated clout."

"That makes it more challenging. But we have an advantage in that we know the people involved. We might be able to get more information than the police because they trust us." Claire settled back on the bench. "So, let's see. We know Zoila argued with Norma and then went to the meditation garden. But we don't know if she had a stop in between."

"We could ask Norma if she knew where Zoila went after the argument," Dom offered.

Claire tilted her head. "We could, but she might not tell us. For some reason, she is being exceedingly closed-mouthed. We should ask around to see if anyone was up at the zen garden that morning, and if they saw anything."

"I talked to Banes." Dom told Claire about his conversation with the groundskeeper and the bag from *Chowders*.

"It sounds like you think the bag from *Chowders* could be significant? Why is that?"

"Banes said the kids leave trash sometimes, but I don't think kids would have a take-out bag from *Chowders*. They usually eat junk food."

Claire scrunched up her face at him. "So, you think the killer ate at *Chowders*?"

"Not necessarily. I talked to Shane and Sarah after Kenneth, and they acted very strange when I asked about Ben."

"Why would you ask about Ben?"

Claire had shifted in her seat to face him and Dom knew she was going to be upset, but he had to mention the clues as he saw them.

"Kenneth said he was at Zoila's yesterday and I know he does delivery for *Chowders*. There was a *Chowders* bag up near the crime scene..." Dom shrugged, letting his voice trail off.

"Ben wouldn't leave trash up there!"

"Not normally ... but if he was fleeing a murder scene, he might."

Claire's cheeks burned. Her face turned incredulous as she stared at Dom. "You can't seriously suspect Ben? You know he couldn't kill anyone and I can assure you from a psychological standpoint, he's not capable. Besides, *why* would Ben want to kill Zoila?"

"That's the big question. Why would anyone. If we could answer that, we'd have our killer. Besides, it seems that Ben has an alibi."

"He does?"

"Yes, Sarah said he visits his mother on the mainland on Wednesdays and I don't think he would have been on the island when she was killed."

That's right, Claire thought. How had she forgotten that? Of course Ben could not have done it. She felt a pang of worry—she'd noticed herself getting more and more forgetful and hoped it was just a normal sign of aging and not something more sinister.

"Right. Well, I can assure you it wasn't Ben or Norma," Claire said in a clipped tone. Then, she calmed down and gave the situation some thought. It was better to act professionally, not emotionally. "We need some more leads to follow. Are you sure Banes didn't see anyone else up there or hear anything? You'd think Zoila would have screamed."

"No. He was cleaning up horse poop on the trails and he said he doesn't hear very good," Dom said. "As far as I know, no one else has come forward to say they were there that morning."

"*Meow!*"

Dom looked down to see a large Maine Coon cat weaving in between Claire's ankles. Claire reached down to pet the cat's head.

"Is that your cat?" Dom asked.

"No. She's a stray, but she comes to my garden sometimes, and I always leave something out for her. I call her Porch Cat."

"Oh. I've seen her on my patio. I wondered who owned her. She seems to stroll by in the afternoon, most days." Dom tossed a pistachio to the cat. She looked up at him with suspicious green eyes, sniffed the pistachio disdainfully, then rubbed the side of her head on Claire's calf while she presented Dom with her back end.

Claire laughed. "I guess she doesn't like pistachios. I think most of the neighbors feed her —she's well fed. I think she makes the rounds, and I've seen her sunning herself in the gardens up at the conservation area."

"Near the zen garden?"

"Yes. Too bad she can't talk," Claire said. "She probably knows a lot about what's going on around the island. She might even know who killed Zoila."

"*Meow!*" The cat looked up at Claire, then glared at Dom before continuing on her path along the length of the dock.

"That's exactly what we need. Someone who might have seen something but didn't realize it was important, so they didn't come forward," Dom said.

"Yeah. But preferably someone who can actually talk," Claire replied.

Dom watched the cat amble lazily down the wooden dock toward the shops, thinking what a great source of information it would be, with the run of the island and no one censoring their conversations around her. The cat would be privy to all sorts of information.

A light blinked in Dom's brain, and he thought of someone else who might be in a similar situation but could actually communicate with them. "Kenneth said the Flannery kid rode his bike past Zoila's yesterday on his way through the conservation area. Do the kids ride through there a lot?"

"I think so. I remember Robby saying he has to give them a talking to a lot because the bikes are wearing down the paths."

"Maybe one of them saw something and was too scared to say so, or didn't realize it might be significant," Dom suggested.

"Could be. We should definitely ask around," Claire agreed. "If I was being called in as a consultant, I'd know exactly what to do next. But now that we aren't with the police, things need to be handled differently. What do you suggest we do?"

Dom was glad Claire was asking his opinion instead of dictating the tasks. Maybe this partnership would work out, after all. "I say we talk to Norma and find out just what Zambuco is up to. We might be able to figure out what he is thinking and anticipate his next move by the questions he asked her. Maybe you can talk to your nephew and see if he will give us any insider information on the case."

"Sure, I can do that. I don't know what he'll share with me, but every little bit helps and I feel like we better get to the bottom of this ourselves before Zambuco comes up with the wrong conclusion and arrests the wrong person."

"And the real killer gets off scot-free." Dom glanced over at the shops in time to see Mae coming out of the fish store with a brown paper package in her hand. Apparently, she'd traded jam for fish. Life was going on as normal here on Mooseamuck Island—the islanders seemed to be unconcerned that a killer was running around loose.

An icy finger danced up his spine, causing an involuntary shiver as Dom wondered if Zoila would be the only victim, or if the killer was already busy planning his next murder.

Chapter Twelve

"And what do you two want?" Norma glared from her desk at Dom and Claire, who stood just inside the doorway of her studio.

"We're trying to help you," Claire said softly. "Zambuco's coming by. He found out you had a fight with Zoila."

"Already been by," Norma snapped. "Asked a lot of annoying questions, just like you did."

Dom stepped inside the small studio and Claire followed behind him, then shut the door. The sun filtered in from the large window in the front, highlighting the bright colors of Norma's paintings that hung on every inch of wall space. The closed-in space intensified the smell of oil and turpentine, and Dom stifled a sneeze. "What, exactly, did he ask?"

Norma waved her hand in the air dismissively. "Oh, you know. Where was I this morning? What did I fight with Zoila about? Did I kill her? The usual interrogation stuff."

"And what did you tell him?" Dom asked.

"I told him it was none of his business, just like it's none of yours."

Claire flapped her hands against her sides in frustration. "We're just trying to help. If you tell us what this is all about, we can try to figure out who the killer is and get Zambuco off your back. But when you remain silent like this, you're making it seem like you *did* kill Zoila."

Norma pushed herself up from her desk and took a few steps toward them. Dom looked down at her feet and noticed she wore men's work boots with round toes. The image of the footprint left in the sand at the zen garden drifted to his mind.

"Is that what you think?" Norma thumped her cane on the floor loudly. "That I killed her?"

"No, of course not," Claire soothed.

"Well, I didn't." Norma crossed her arms over her chest. "But I'm also not going to tell anyone what the argument was about or where I went. That information is confidential."

Dom and Claire exchanged a frustrated glance.

"Can you at least tell us what you think Zambuco was getting at? Did he mention any evidence or what he thought a motive might be?" Dom asked.

"He seemed to think that Zoila might have seen something in one of her readings. Some sort of premonition, and whatever it was, someone didn't want her talking about it."

"Is that what you were arguing about? A premonition she had?"

Norma shook her head. "No. And I'm not exactly sure Zambuco is barking up the right tree.

See, Zoila had made a strange discovery, and if it was true ... well, let's just say there's someone on the island who might not like it very much."

Dom's eyebrows tingled. "Enough to kill her?"

"Maybe." Norma glanced out the window and Claire's heart twisted as she noticed Norma's eyes were moist. Was she about to cry? She'd never known the older woman to shed a tear before.

Claire reached out and rubbed Norma's arm. "Then why don't you tell us what it is? We can help."

Norma pressed her lips together, then looked at Claire with clear, determined eyes. "I wish I could, but sometimes one has to honor their word above all. Even if it means becoming a murder suspect."

***

"Well, that wasn't very helpful," Dom said as they walked down the sidewalk past the quaint Crab Cove shops after leaving Norma's studio.

Claire chewed her bottom lip. "Why won't she tell us? It doesn't make sense. Is she covering for someone?"

"Maybe she is trying to throw up a smoke screen."

"You mean like to throw us off track? Why would she do that if she wasn't guilty?" Claire stopped walking and looked over at Dom. "You don't really think it *is* her, do you?"

Dom looked up. Two gulls flew overhead, their raucous cries piercing the air. "A lot of the clues do point to her, but still, I can't see it. And there's too many unanswered questions. We need to find out what was on that paper and where it is now."

"Not to mention the murder weapon."

"And the footprint. I couldn't tell what kind of shoe it was, but it looked like a large boot with a rounded toe."

"A man's boot?" Claire asked hopefully.

"It could be either, and let's not forget some women wear men's boots." Dom glanced back at Norma's studio.

Claire's phone burst out in eerie science fiction music, and they both jumped. Cell phone reception was spotty on the island and they weren't used to phones blaring out at random times. She pulled it out and looked at the caller ID. "It's Robby. I'd better answer it."

Claire walked away a few paces, and Dom stared out at the harbor. The scene usually calmed his nerves, but it wasn't very calming now. Too many thoughts were clamoring for attention in his head. And a murderer was on the loose. He noticed the ferry pulling up to the dock. Just as they had suspected, Zambuco wasn't able to stop the ferries for long, which meant the killer could have easily slipped off the island. That might make finding him harder unless the killer was an islander, because if it was, their absence would soon become suspicious. Everyone knew everyone else's habits on Mooseamuck Island, and if someone deviated from the norm, there was sure to be talk about it.

Claire joined him again, her face grim.

"Did he tell you anything of interest?" Dom asked.

"He was reluctant to divulge too much information, but I did manage to get one clue about the footprint out of him. I had to promise to bake him an apple pie, though."

"Oh? What was the clue?" Dom's eyebrows started to tingle, and he unconsciously smoothed them with his fingertips.

"They couldn't make out the model of shoe, but they did find some interesting tiny pieces of shell in the impression. Jonah crab shell."

Dom's high hopes deflated, and his eyebrows stopped tingling. "Crab shell? I hardly think that will help narrow things down. This place is loaded with crabs. That's why it's called Crab Cove."

"Not Jonah crabs. Those are only found in one remote place on the island. It's off the beaten path so hardly anyone ever goes there, but it has a nice view of the lighthouse and I know one person who manages a visit at least once a week."

"Oh, really?" The tingling started up again. Dom didn't need to ask who the person was, but he did anyway. "Who?"

"Norma."

Chapter Thirteen

Claire thought about Zoila's murder as she pinched the spent blooms from the purple petunia that hung from her back porch. The sun was just starting to set behind her as she took her last look of the day out over the Atlantic. It was unusually calm, which Claire thought was funny given the hectic events on the island.

Her thoughts turned to the information Robby had given her and her gut tightened. Just because there were crab shells in the shoe imprint *and* Norma was known to go to that stretch of the island didn't mean she was the killer. Lots of people wore work boots with round toes. And lots of people could have gone there, though Claire knew most people didn't bother because the beach was all rocky and there were nicer places that were easier to get to.

Norma had implied someone else might want to silence Zoila ... but who? And why wouldn't Norma tell them? It didn't make sense. Norma knew something, and the fact that she wouldn't tell anyone didn't bode well for her.

"Meow."

Claire looked down to see the stray Maine Coon looking up at her with curious, green eyes.

The cat had something in its mouth and Claire bent down to see what it was.

"Hi, there." Claire rubbed between the cat's ears and was rewarded with a loud purring. The cat spit out the object—a shiny green leaf. Claire picked it up and then turned it over curiously.

"Where'd you get this?" she wondered. It was a smooth, winterberry holly leaf. The plant was very rare in this part of Maine. In fact, Claire knew of only one place that it grew. "Have you been to Anna's garden?"

"*Meow.*"

Claire stood with the leaf still in her hand. Anna Campbell was an avid gardener, just like Claire—at least she had been, before cancer made her so weak she couldn't do anything but lay in bed. Thinking of Anna, who lay in hospice on the mainland with only a few weeks—maybe even days—left to live, reminded her of Ben and her heart clenched for him.

She thought about how Ben's name kept coming up in the investigation. That had to be a coincidence—Claire was sure sweet, simple Ben couldn't be involved.

Dom had said that Sarah and Shane acted strange when he asked them about Ben, and Kenneth had seen Ben speeding away from Zoila's. She rubbed the smooth leaf in between her thumb and forefinger, her forehead creasing with worry. Ben was under a lot of pressure, with his mother being sick and off the island. That pressure could make him act strangely ... but murder? No. Claire didn't think so. He would have no reason to kill Zoila.

Claire knew Anna and Norma were best friends. In fact, Norma had promised Anna she would look after Ben once Anna was gone. Though Ben was a grown man in his fifties and could function on his own for the most part, his simple outlook and limited capabilities sometimes made people think they could take advantage of him. Norma would protect him from that ... but was she protecting him now?

There had to be more to it. Something was going on, but Claire was sure neither Norma nor Ben had anything to do with Zoila's death. She needed to find out who was up at the zen garden that morning, and it looked like her best bet was to talk to some of the kids around town and see if they'd noticed anyone. She made a mental note to seek them out before she met Dom at *Chowders* in the morning.

"*Meow!*"

Claire looked down to see the cat sitting at her door expectantly.

"Oh, I see. You're looking for your saucer of milk, are you?"

The cat flicked its ears and looked from Claire to the door, and back to Claire.

Claire laughed. "Okay, you win."

She went inside and poured some milk into a small bowl, which she left outside for the cat to drink at her leisure. She considered inviting the cat inside, but she never seemed to want to come in. Maybe when the weather got colder she would accept the invitation. It might be nice to have another living creature in the house to snuggle with on the long winter nights.

Claire snapped on the light beside her favorite oversized chair that sat next to the big stone fireplace in the sitting room of her cottage. It was too warm for a fire, but sitting next to the hearth made her feel cozy.

She picked up the crossword puzzle she'd been working on and settled into the chair, grabbing her half-moon reading glasses from the side-table. Then she opened the drawer of the table and peeked inside hopefully. She was in luck—a tiny piece of dark chocolate sat inside the drawer, right where she'd hidden it. She picked the piece out and unwrapped it, savoring the slightly bitter taste of the chocolate. It was an indulgence she allowed herself because of the many health

116

benefits, and she often placed small squares of chocolate in various places around the house, usually forgetting just where she'd put them. It was always a nice surprise to find one.

She finished the chocolate and turned her attention to the crossword. Just a few more words and it would be complete. Then she would turn in early ... she needed to get a head start tomorrow if she wanted to get ahead of Zambuco before he came to the wrong conclusion.

***

Further up Israel Head Hill, Dom sat in his kitchen, a plate of ravioli on the table in front of him. He'd tried his hand at making them ... rolling out the pasta dough and placing a spoonful of ricotta filling inside. They weren't as good as his Nonna's or Sophia's, but they were okay.

He ate carefully, cutting each ravioli exactly in half, and eating one half then the next while he reflected on the events of the day. Working with Claire might not be so bad. Sure, she used emotion too much, but he had to admit getting an insight into how people thought and what motivated them to act a certain way could be fascinating. And she did come in handy given her connection to the police, even though Robby hadn't given them too many good clues.

He thought about the one clue they did get—the crab shells found in the footprint impression. Something didn't sit right with that. How could they know for sure who had been to that part of the island? Dom wasn't sure if the footprint was too smudged to be able to pinpoint the exact size and model of shoe. He'd have to wait to find out.

A chattering from the birdcage caught Dom's attention and he looked up to see Romeo preening Juliet's aqua and white feathers. A feeling of sadness descended on him—the birds reminded him of what he'd lost when Sophia died.

He balanced the last piece of ravioli on his fork and brought it to his mouth. No sense in looking back. Sophia was gone now, and he'd better make the best of the rest of his life, just like he'd promised her he would. And besides, he did have something to look forward to—Zoila's murder case. For the first time in years, he felt hopeful again, as if a dark shroud was being lifted and he could finally see clearly. He just hoped he was up for the task.

His eyebrows tingled, and he smoothed them out as he thought about the many questions yet to be answered.

What was Norma hiding?

Why had Sarah and Shane acted so strangely?

Was Ben involved somehow?

Most importantly, what had Zoila discovered that someone wanted so desperately to keep quiet that they killed her?

Another disturbing thought poked into Dom's mind—Zoila might have told someone what she'd discovered and, if that was the case, the killer's work might not yet be done.

Romeo scuttled over to the edge of his cage and watched Dom intently.

"Are you looking for a treat?" Dom picked a small piece of spinach out of his salad bowl, taking care to make sure it had no dressing on it, and held it up to the cage.

Romeo looked sideways at the spinach with his bright, black eyes, and then reached over with his tiny beak and pulled the leaf through the cage. He chewed it quickly, then flew to the side of the cage, clinging onto the grates and looking right at Dom.

"*Burber Peepon*," he squawked.

Dom smiled. Romeo's words were getting easier for him to understand, but he wasn't sure if it was because the bird was talking better or his ear was becoming more accustomed to the sounds. Either way, the bird had an uncanny way of saying the right word at the right time.

"That's right, my little friend." Dom fed another piece of spinach to the bird. "We have yet to find the murder weapon … and when we do, will it lead us to the murderer?"

Chapter Fourteen

Chowders was abuzz with locals finishing up their breakfast when Claire slipped into the seat across the Formica table from Jane the next morning.

"Morning." Jane slid a tea cup in front of Claire. "Where have you been?"

"I was talking to some of the island kids." Claire glanced down the table and nodded at Dom, who tipped his coffee cup toward her in acknowledgment.

Beside her, Alice's knitting needles stopped clacking. "About the murder?" Did one of them see something?"

"Unfortunately, no." Claire shrugged and glanced at Dom. "Just Ben joyriding down the trails."

"Joy riding?" Mae's brows puckered together. "Ben's usually so careful. I haven't known him to go fast down those trails. It's dangerous."

"Maybe he's getting reckless with his worry for Anna," Tom suggested.

The table fell silent as they all thought about Anna, and how her death would affect Ben.

"I guess it's up to us to look after Ben now," Alice said. "Along with Norma, of course."

"I heard Zambuco searched Norma's place last night," Mae added.

Claire's heart pinched. "Searched it? For what?"

Mae shrugged. "Evidence, I guess. Maybe the murder weapon. I heard they haven't found that yet."

Tom Landry frowned at Mae. "Surely, you don't think Norma did it, do you?"

"Of course not." Mae gave him a disgusted glare, then turned to Dom and Claire. "What do you guys think? You *are* investigating it, aren't you?"

Claire looked at Dom. What *did* they think? Usually, they wouldn't discuss clues with anyone during an ongoing investigation, but this one was different. They weren't officially working with the police. Still, she didn't know how much they should share. Then again, they didn't have much information to share, anyway.

Alice's knitting needles clacked away as she looked at them slyly. "I heard from Velma that you two had teamed up, just like when you used to work together before."

"We have, but we really don't know much," Claire sighed.

"Well, who are your suspects?" Mae looked from Dom to Claire expectantly.

Dom cleared his throat. "We don't actually have any suspects. We've been trying to reconstruct the events of the day. Do any of you happen to know where Zoila went or who she met with that morning or the day before?"

Mae, Tom, Jane and Alice looked at each other and shrugged.

"Well, both Kenneth and Shane said they were at Zoila's the day before yesterday." Mae tilted her head toward the counter to jog their memories of the previous days conversation.

"And we know Norma and Zoila had ... umm ... words ... yesterday morning," Tom added.

"Other than that, I don't know Zoila's schedule. Did you guys get a copy of her appointment book?" Mae asked.

"Unfortunately, only the police are privy to that information," Claire answered.

"Then seems to be you ought to be out following that detective Zambuco around and seeing who he talks to. He's bound to be talking to the people in that book. Those would be his suspects," Mae said.

"Right." Claire bristled with annoyance. She didn't need Mae Biddeford telling her how to investigate a murder. "We talked to Norma right after Zambuco yesterday to try to find out his line of reasoning."

"And?" Jane's brows rose over her steaming cup of chai tea.

"Norma is being very tight-lipped," Claire said. "It's hard to say what Zambuco was thinking. But we should get going and see what he's up to today."

Claire stood and fished in her pocket for some money. Dom followed suit.

"And I guess we should talk to Ben, since he was seen racing away from the gardens yesterday morning," Dom added.

Jane pressed her lips together. "Ben? He wouldn't have been there yesterday morning."

"Why not?" Dom asked.

"He visits his mother on the mainland on Wednesdays."

"Oh, that's right." Claire glanced over at the counter, caught Sarah's eye and waved her over. "It will be easy to just verify that by asking. The kids probably made a mistake—you know how kids are."

"Can I get you guys something else?" Sarah stood at the end of the table.

"Oh, no, I was just wondering if Ben was around. I have a question for him," Claire said.

Sarah's eyes flicked toward the back room, then toward the door, then back to Claire. She shuffled her feet. "Why would you have a question for Ben?"

"I just wanted—"

But Claire didn't get to finish the sentence, because just then the door burst open and Hazel came running in, her face flushed and eyes wide.

Silence fell over the diner as everyone stopped what they were doing to stare at the elderly innkeeper, who stood in the doorway wringing her hands.

"You guys won't believe it—Norma's been arrested for the murder of Zoila Rivers!"

Chapter Fifteen

Claire ripped open the door to the Mooseamuck Island police station and stormed up to the counter. Behind it, Gail Waller looked at her with large eyes.

"Hi, Claire. Is something wr—"

"I want to see Robby right now," Claire demanded, cutting her off.

Gail pushed up from the desk and scurried down the hall, bumping into Robby who was just entering the front room.

"What's going on?" Claire frowned at her nephew. "Did you arrest Norma?"

Robby's face hardened. "Zambuco did, but she's being held here."

"On what grounds? Do you have enough evidence?"

Robby skirted around the counter to stand beside her. He put his hand on her shoulder and escorted her and Dom, who had been standing silently at her side, to the row of orange plastic chairs that sat along one wall.

Robby pushed the irate Claire into a chair and sat beside her. "He does have evidence."

"Like what?" Claire asked.

Robby's face hardened. "You know I can't discuss that with you."

"The murder weapon?" Claire persisted.

"No. We haven't found that yet. She might have tossed it in the ocean."

"Well, then I don't see how you can make a case." Claire glanced at Dom who nodded his agreement.

"Unless there was a witness?" Dom suggested.

Robby shook his head. "No. I can't say any more, but I agree with Zambuco that this is the best course of action."

"What?" Claire pushed out of her seat, flapping her arms in frustration. "How could it be best? You know Norma is no killer."

"You have to trust the justice system," Robby said.

"Well, if this is the kind of system we have on the island, I think I'll consider moving." Claire spat out the words, then crossed her arms over her chest with a sigh. "Can we at least see her?"

"They've just finished processing her. I can take you back." Robby stood and walked toward the back, with Claire and Dom following.

The Mooseamuck Island Police Station was small, occupying an area in the basement of the town hall which they shared with the public works department, so they didn't have far to go. Claire followed Robby down a short hallway that led to the two jail cells. Norma was in one, the other was empty.

Norma looked up as they entered the room, a scowl on her face.

"What do you two want?"

Claire's heart pinched. She could tell the scowl and harsh words were just a front. Or at least she thought so.

"We're here to help. We know you didn't kill Zoila," Claire said.

After a moment of silence from Norma, Dom added. "Did you?"

"Of course not."

Claire turned to Robby. "Why does she have to stay in jail? She hasn't been convicted or anything and just what, exactly, is the evidence, anyway?"

Robby sighed and ticked off the items with his fingers. "Well, she was seen fighting with the victim. She fled the island. And she won't tell us a thing. Usually, that all adds up to guilty."

Norma harrumphed, jamming her cane loudly on the floor.

"Norma, why won't you tell us about the fight and clear yourself from this bogus charge?"

"Well, I don't know if that would clear me and besides, I can't tell you. It's not for me to tell."

Robby shrugged. "If she won't help herself, I can't help her. She needs a lawyer who can get her out on bail. In the meantime, Zambuco has agreed to let her stay here instead of sending her over to the big jail on the mainland."

Claire gripped the bars of the cell with her fingers. "We'll get you a lawyer and get you out of here."

Norma simply shrugged, pulled a pencil out from behind her ear and started sketching on a napkin that sat on her lunch tray.

Claire tried one last time. "Norma, I wish you would think about at least telling me and Dom what went on between you and Zoila. We won't tell anyone, and it could give us a clue that might help us find the real killer."

Norma shook her head, her eyes never leaving the napkin. "I can't *say* what it was. Some trusts cannot be broken. Anyway, it's not so bad in here. I get three free meals a day and would probably be able to catch up on some rest if everyone would leave me alone."

Claire sighed as she watched Norma's pencil work furiously. "Can you at least tell us what was on that piece of paper she had?"

Norma looked up from her sketch. "I'm not going to tell and that's final. You need to run along now—all of you. But remember, murder cases can be like an impressionist painting—

sometimes, if you are standing too close, you can't really see the whole scene."

Leave it to Norma to wave off help and then say something cryptic, Claire thought as she glanced down at the napkin before turning away. She was surprised at how quickly Norma had worked up an amazingly realistic sketch. There was a background of pine trees and scrub brush, then, nestled in a clearing, an old cabin with a tall stone chimney—Zoila's cabin.

***

"I just don't understand what is wrong with her," Claire said as they left the police station. "And I don't see how Zambuco could have arrested her ... I mean, don't they need something more solid than that flimsy evidence Robby mentioned?"

Dom nodded. "Yes, it does seem a bit premature."

"But I guess if I didn't know Norma so well, I would say the clues *did* point in her direction."

"True, but clues can also be deceiving."

Claire glanced sideways at Dom. She'd always thought he considered clues to be cut and dried. Perhaps there was another side to him that she hadn't seen before. "What do you mean?"

"Well ... I can't be sure ... but I have a theory." He preened his eyebrows. Then he shook his head. "No, I can't say anything until I can prove it."

Claire studied him. He was on to something, but she knew from experience she wouldn't be able to get a thing out of him until he was ready. She stood at her car door and replayed their talk with Norma in her head while she waited for Dom to get in the passenger side.

"What she said at the end—about the impressionist painting—do you think that was some kind of clue?" she asked Dom over the roof of the Fiat.

"I think she might have been *sketching* us a clue." Dom opened the door and slid into the passenger seat while Claire got into the driver's seat.

"You mean the hunting camp?"

Dom nodded.

"But Zoila wasn't killed there." Claire started the car but didn't put it into gear—she was too interested in hearing Dom's theory on Norma's sketch.

"We already know where she was killed, so that wouldn't have been much of a clue," Dom pointed out.

"But how could the hunting camp be a clue?"

Dom shrugged. "Maybe it started there. The argument with the killer. Or maybe there is a clue still there to be found."

Claire's brows crept up. "That could be. But how would we get in? The police must have it locked up tight."

"Maybe we need to look at it from another angle. Who do we know who was at the camp before she died?"

Claire pressed her lips together and thought. "Well, Kenneth and Shane were both there the day before she died. They said so at the diner that morning."

"That's right." Dom remembered the sand he felt under his feet at the counter that morning after Shane left. Could that sand have come from the zen garden? He pictured his later visit when Shane had been fixing the oven, his round-toed work boots in clear view. "And Sarah and Shane acted awfully jumpy when I asked about Ben."

"You know, I hate to say it, but I've always felt like Sarah was hiding something."

"What do you mean?"

"I don't know. Something about her past," Claire hesitated. "She just kind of has an air about her like she has some kind of secret she doesn't want anyone to know."

Dom nodded, much to Claire's surprise. "I noticed that, too."

"You don't think she could have anything to do with it? I don't even think she knew Zoila."

"*She* might not have known Zoila ... but maybe Zoila knew *her*."

"Or her secret."

Chapter Sixteen

Claire and Dom knew from experience that they couldn't just ask Sarah about her secret ... especially if it had something to do with Zoila's murder. Even if it didn't, she clearly didn't want anyone to know about it, so they doubted direct questioning would yield any results.

They took a more indirect route. Claire researched her on the internet, and Dom discreetly tried to find out her whereabouts on the morning of the murder.

They agreed to spend a few hours on their tasks and meet at a small coffee shop in the cove to discuss their findings at two p.m. Which is exactly where Claire was sitting with her hand wrapped around a steaming mug of green tea when Dom walked in the door.

He nodded at Claire, then paid for a coffee which he poured from the self-serve carafes before sliding into the booth opposite her.

"How'd you make out?" he asked without preamble.

Claire shook her head. "Not good. Or maybe it was good, depending on how you look at it."

Dom raised a brow and Claire continued.

"I did a search on Sarah White, starting with Lowell Massachusetts where she claims to be from, and the only person living there with that name during that timeframe is eighty-seven years old!"

"Well, that can't be her. But maybe you got the town wrong." Dom sipped his coffee. "Or maybe she lived in a smaller town near Lowell. Sometimes people say they are from the next biggest town because others don't recognize the smaller town names."

"I thought of that. There are no Sarah Whites that fit the description in any surrounding towns."

Dom pressed his lips together. "Well, that certainly does raise suspicions. However, Sarah could not have murdered Zoila."

Claire didn't know whether to be glad or depressed about that. She liked Sarah and didn't want her to be the killer, but if it wasn't her, then who did they have left as suspects?

"Why not?"

"I checked around and she was at *Chowders* all morning. Several witnesses say she was there as early as six a.m. And since you saw Zoila alive at six, that means she was killed some time after six, so it couldn't have been Sarah who killed her."

Claire stared out the window. The cove waters across the street were dappled with sunlight. Tourists in colorful clothes walked by with shopping bags dangling from their hands. They were happy, smiling. Claire sighed and turned her attention back to her tea. She was in no mood to see happy people.

"So, Sarah has an alibi. But she also has a secret ... and it must be important, seeing as she seems to be lying about who she really is." Claire looked up at Dom. "So, if she didn't do it, maybe someone did it for her."

"Someone who cares enough about her to kill for her?" Dom asked.

Claire nodded.

"Well, I noticed Shane seems to be pretty sweet on her." Dom lowered his voice. "And I felt sand on the floor in the diner at the counter, right where he had been standing the morning of the murder."

"You think he might have been the one who left the footprint in the zen garden?"

Dom shrugged. "Maybe."

"But he seemed so surprised when he found out Zoila had been killed."

"Maybe he's a good actor. We've seen killers act surprised before."

It was true—even the most hardened killers seemed to be able to pull off an award-winning performance when it came to diverting suspicion. But Shane wasn't a hardened killer ... she'd known his family since he was a baby. Then again, they'd also seen love make people do crazy things ... including murder.

Claire didn't want to say it out loud, but Shane wasn't the only one who cared about Sarah. She knew Sarah and Ben had grown very close since Sarah came to the island. Especially after Anna got sick. Sarah had been almost like a sister to him. She'd encouraged him to take the delivery job and that had given Ben much-needed self-esteem. Claire knew Ben looked up to Sarah ... but would he kill for her?

"We need to find out Zoila's time of death and then figure out if Shane had opportunity." Claire eyed her phone, noticing there was no reception, as usual. "Maybe I can get that information from Robby."

"If he's feeling generous, maybe you can get him to tell us the exact make and size of shoe that made that footprint and if there was any distinguishing tread wear," Dom said.

"I'll try."

"There's something else strange." Dom rubbed his eyebrows. "Shane's account of when he was at Zoila's doesn't match with Kenneth's. Kenneth said he saw Shane around one o'clock, but Shane said he was there after three."

"Why would Shane lie about that?" Claire asked. "Zoila wasn't killed until the next day, so it's not like he would lie so as to not be placed at the scene of the crime."

"Not *that* crime," Dom said. "But maybe there was something else that happened at Zoila's that he didn't want to be implicated in."

"Like what?"

"I have no idea. Perhaps that will come out as we investigate further. I do know one thing, though. We need to take a trip out to Zoila's and see if there's anything out there that might yield a clue."

Claire looked down into her empty cup. "But it's probably locked up and on this case, we don't have the benefit of being able to just browse around the properties that the police have secured."

"That's unfortunate. But we can still go out and take a look around outside ... maybe even peek in the windows. One never knows what one might find. "Dom pushed himself up from his chair and looked at Claire expectantly. "You game?"

***

Claire had been out to the old hunting camp many times before in her youth, but today, it looked different. She eyed it ominously as they drive slowly up the dirt road where it sat shrouded in the darkness of the forest trees, enveloped in the stillness of death.

That's silly, she thought as she hopped out of Dom's Smart Car. It was just her imagination running wild, applying emotions to the camp knowing the owner was now dead. The camp was an inanimate object—no more menacing now than it had been before Zoila's murder.

The rustic, log exterior blended perfectly with the deep-woods setting. Darkened windows glared at Claire as they approached the wide porch that ran along the front of the house.

Dom reached out and twisted the knob on the thick, oak door. "It's locked."

"Not surprised." Claire cupped her hand over her eyes and peered through the window next to the door into the living room. Zoila had decorated it comfortably with a leather sofa facing the oversized stone fireplace. Claire wondered if the granny-square afghan draped over the back of the sofa was one of Alice's creations. An oval, braided rug lay in the center of the tidy room. Claire felt a tug of sadness as she looked, in realizing that when Zoila left the cabin on Wednesday morning, she never realized it would be for the last time.

"Do you see anything of interest?" Dom moved to the window at the end of the porch, cupping his own hands over his eyes to look in.

"Not really." Claire noticed a few stones had come loose from the side of the chimney and were lying on the hearth. "The chimney looks like it needs some repair, but didn't Shane say that was part of what she was having redone?"

"Yep." Dom was already off the porch and circling the house. From the side, Claire could see the various add-ons that had been built over the years. The different siding and architectural styles made them obvious. They peered into windows as they went around, but nothing seemed amiss.

Behind the camp was an old toolshed. Dom lifted the latch and the door squealed open.

"At least we can get in here," Claire said as she surveyed the small shed full of gardening equipment, old tires, a snowblower and even a baby carriage that looked like it was from the early 1900s.

"I guess the Barretts left some of their stuff here after they sold the place." Dom took down a rake that had been hanging on the side of the wall and looked it over, reminding Claire that the murder weapon—which they presumed was the rake from the zen garden—was still missing.

Dom smiled ruefully as he noticed her attention to the rake. "Wrong kind."

"Just as well. It would be very strange for the murder weapon to show up here in Zoila's tool shed when she'd been murdered in the zen garden."

"True, but maybe our killer is very clever. It's the last place anyone would look."

Claire nodded, her attention drifting to a stack of old, framed pictures leaning against the side of the shed. "Looks like they even left old pictures."

Dom came to stand beside her, pointing to the smudged dust in the middle of the tops of the frames. "It looks like someone has handled these recently."

"Maybe Zoila moved them from the house for the renovations," Claire suggested.

"Kenneth said Zoila had called him over to pick up some family pictures. I wonder why he didn't take them."

Claire held up a framed photograph that looked to be about seventy years old. "I know why. Kenneth didn't get along with his father."

Dom's brow creased and he pointed to a handsome young man in the photo. "Is this his father?"

Claire nodded. "His name was Silas. He died a few years ago."

"I see the resemblance," Dom said as he studied the image of the man. Even though the picture was in black and white, he could tell the man had the same blond hair and preppy looks as Kenneth, right down to the dimple on his chin. "He seems kind of old to be Kenneth's father. Isn't Kenneth only in his forties?"

"He had Kenneth late in life. I guess he was too busy making money to take a wife. Kenneth's mother was a lot younger."

Dom was quiet while he studied the picture for a few seconds. "Who are the others?"

Claire looked at the picture again, then laughed. "You won't believe it, but this is Norma and the woman next to her is Anna Campbell."

"Ben's mother?" Dom looked at the picture. Now that Claire had pointed it out, he recognized a younger and less grumpy Norma. She stood next to a woman who was a true beauty. Silas stood on the other side of the woman, looking at her with a bemused smile on his face as if she'd just said something clever. "They look like good friends."

"I guess they were, back in the day. That was before Silas took over the family business. Norma said he changed after that and they didn't hang around together anymore, but she and Anna remained best friends."

Dom put the photo down and thumbed through the others. They were old family portraits, some in oil paint. He noticed one in an elaborate gold frame that had the paper backing torn at the top. The man immortalized by the painting had the Barrett blonde hair and dimple.

"That's Kenneth's grandfather. Jeb Barrett," Claire said.

"I see the resemblance," Dom sighed, and carefully placed the picture back with the others. "Unfortunately, there's no clue here as to why Shane ... or anyone else ... would want to kill Zoila."

"I'm not really convinced Shane had anything to do with it," Claire said as they shut the shed door and started toward the car. "As you saw, the fireplace does need repair so he did have a legitimate reason to be here."

"Well, if we want to clear Norma, we have to start eliminating the suspects and see where it leads us."

"I guess Shane *is* one of our suspects." Claire picked up her cell phone and glanced at the bars. "Still no service. I'll text Robby about the footprint and time of death and hope it goes through when we get back in range."

Dom turned the car around and started down the dirt road that served as the cabin's driveway while Claire formulated her text. Glancing in the rearview mirror at the house and then the shed, he felt his left eyebrow tingle. He patted it with his index finger, then turned his attention to the road ahead of him. "Back in the day, we would have proceeded by figuring out where each suspect was at the time of the murder so we could narrow it down."

"Yeah, and back in the day we'd have been able to haul them into the station for questioning."

"True. We might have to use a more indirect method now."

"You mean like asking around? The Mooseamuck Island grapevine knows everything that is going on around town."

"Yes, that could help." Dom glanced in his rear-view mirror to see a familiar car traveling about a half-mile behind them. "I already asked him where he was and now we just need to verify that."

"Great. Where was he?" Claire checked her phone again. One bar.

"He said he was at the Dumonts'."

"Perfect. I know Ginny very well. I'll just call her up and verify." Another bar popped up and Claire dialed Ginny's number.

"Aloha!"

Claire laughed. "Well, you're in a good mood."

"Who wouldn't be in paradise."

"Paradise?"

"Yes, didn't you know? We're on vacation in Hawaii!"

Oh." Claire's brow wrinkled. "I didn't know about that. Are you having work done on your house while you're away?"

"Shane is repointing our chimney, but not this week. We don't want anyone there until we come back. We gave him explicit instructions." Ginny's voice took on a flat tone. "Why, was he there?"

"Oh, no. I was just wondering." Claire caught Dom's sideways glance and asked one last question. "So, you've been away all week?"

"Yep, since Saturday. We're coming back next Wednesday."

"Okay." Claire tried to sound cheerful. "Well, have a nice vacation!"

Claire's stomach sank as she hung up the phone.

"What did she say?" Dom asked.

"Shane wasn't there ... or at least he wasn't supposed to be there. The Dumonts are on vacation and Ginny said she told him to suspend work until they got back. She didn't want anyone on the property while they were away."

Dom pressed his lips together and glanced in the side view mirror before turning right toward the road that led to Crab Cove. "So he *was* lying to me. I thought so."

"But why would he lie? Do you really think he killed Zoila to protect Sarah's secret?"

"I'm not sure, but we're going to find out."

Chapter Seventeen

"Why do you keep looking in the rearview mirror?" Claire asked as they pulled into the small parking lot next to *Chowders*.

"Someone is following us."

Claire twisted around in her seat. "Who? Where?"

"Oh, he's being rather discreet about it, but I know how to spot a tail." Dom turned off the engine and turned to Claire. "I think it's Zambuco."

"Zambuco? Why would he be following *us*?"

"Maybe he's fresh out of leads and is using us for inspiration."

Claire mashed her brows together. "Fresh out of leads for what? He's already arrested Norma. What would he be investigating?"

"He needs better evidence, don't you think? I'm not even sure how he can justify keeping Norma ... unless he knows something we don't."

Claire glanced over her shoulder as she followed Dom into *Chowders*. She didn't see Zambuco, but if Dom was right, there might be hope for Norma to get released. At least she could be in the comfort of her home while Claire and Dom tracked down the real killer ... who she

149

hoped wasn't standing inside *Chowders* looking out at them right now.

Walking through the lot, her heart grew heavy at the sight of Shane's truck.

"This is good." Dom jerked his head in the direction of the truck. "We'll be able to question both of them at the same time."

Anxiety surged through Claire as Dom opened the door. She was glad the diner was empty of customers—she had a feeling the conversation might get heated.

Sarah was behind the counter, slicing into a golden crusted pie. Shane sat on the other side, a white mug of dark coffee in front of him. Both heads swiveled toward the door. Two sets of eyes narrowed suspiciously, alerting Claire to the fact that Sarah and Shane knew they weren't there on a social visit.

"What brings you two here?" Sarah asked guardedly.

"I'm afraid we have some hard questions to ask," Dom said.

"Like what?" Shane's hand clenched his mug.

"Now, look." Dom leaned against the counter, looking down at Shane. "It's better we ask these questions before Zambuco does. Because he's going to come to the same conclusion sooner or later and I'm sure you'd rather come clean to your friends. Maybe we can help keep Zambuco off your back."

"What are you talking about?" Sarah asked.

"We know you have a secret," Dom said. "Did Zoila find out about it and threaten to tell someone?"

Sarah's eyes widened. "What? No. And besides, it's none of your damn business."

"Now, Sarah," Claire soothed. "We aren't prying into your business. But there was a murder here and we know it wasn't Norma. It's just a matter of time before she's cleared and Zambuco comes looking for anyone with a past."

Sarah crossed her arms over her chest and glared at Claire. "Are you saying that just because I didn't grow up here on the island I'll be suspected of killing Zoila?"

"No. Not because you didn't grow up here." Claire kept her voice unemotional. "Because you're running away from something."

Shane jumped up from his seat. "Hey, now, you wait just a minute. Sarah didn't do anything!"

Sarah put her hand on his arm. Claire's heart pinched as she noticed Sarah's eyes were wet with tears. She felt like a heel.

"How do you know I'm running from something?"

151

Claire shrugged. "I'm a psychologist. I saw the signs."

"But I don't understand why that makes me suspicious."

"Look, I don't know what you have in your past, but if it was something you didn't want anyone to know and Zoila found out about it through her psychic abilities and then threatened to tell people ... well ..." Claire let her voice trail off.

"And that's what you think happened? That I killed her because she found out about my past?"

"No. Not you. We know you have an alibi." Dom turned to Shane. "It's you who's the suspect."

"What?" Sarah and Shane yelled in unison, causing Claire to cringe. She noticed Shane's face was beet red, his hands clenched into fists.

"We know you lied about where you were yesterday morning when Zoila was killed," Dom said. "You told me you were at the Dumonts', but Claire checked with them and they said you weren't working there this week."

Claire chewed her bottom lip. If Shane really was the killer, confronting him like this might not have been a very smart idea. On other cases, they usually had police backup, but they didn't have that now.

She was suddenly very nervous ... if he'd killed once, he might kill again to keep them quiet. But instead of rising up in anger, Shane collapsed in a sigh. Claire noticed him exchange a look with Sarah and wondered if it was true. Had Shane killed for her, and if so, would he confess now and wait quietly for them to call Zambuco?

Sarah shook her head in resignation. "First of all, my past isn't anything I'd kill over and I certainly wouldn't have anyone do my killing for me. It *is* private, though, so I'm not telling anyone, even if you do throw me in jail. And second of all, Shane couldn't have killed Zoila ... he was here all morning that day."

"He was?" Dom's brows tingled as they scrunched into a bushy 'V' in the middle of his forehead. No one had mentioned that Shane was in the restaurant when he'd asked around about Sarah's whereabouts that morning, but then again, he'd only asked about Sarah. It was easy enough to verify later as plenty of people were working that morning, so he doubted they would be lying now. "But why did you lie and say you were at the Dumonts'?"

Sarah and Shane exchanged another glance and Claire thought they *did* have something to hide—it just wasn't something about Zoila.

Shane looked at them sheepishly. "I lied because I was here that morning helping Sarah out in the back. I was covering for Ben."

"Ben?" Claire looked between Sarah and Shane in confusion. "Why would you cover for him?"

"He usually comes in early, before he goes to visit Anna, and does the salad bar," Sarah said. "But that morning, he didn't come in, so Shane helped me out."

"When you asked where I was, I didn't want to mention anything about Ben not coming in, so I just said I was at the first job that popped into my head." Shane looked at Claire ruefully. "Guess I picked the wrong one."

"I don't understand why you would cover for Ben," Dom said. "Didn't you say he called in sick?"

"That's what I *said*, but he actually didn't call in. I just told Zambuco that because I didn't want him to hassle Ben." Sarah turned pleading eyes to Claire. "You know how sensitive he is."

"Yes, of course. Zambuco would scare him silly."

"And of course he couldn't have had anything to do with Zoila's murder." Sarah wrung her hands together, looking not at all certain that what she said was true. "Because he visits his mother over on the mainland on Wednesdays after kitchen duty, so he wouldn't even have been on the island when Zoila was killed."

"Right." Claire nodded, then narrowed her eyes. "So why were the two of you lying and covering up for him, then?"

Shane glanced at Sarah, who nodded slightly.

"When people started asking questions about him, we didn't know what to do. The truth is that no one's seen him since the day before Zoila died," Shane said.

"That's right." Sarah's face twisted in anguish and her next words pinched Claire's heart. "Ben has disappeared."

Chapter Eighteen

"I hate to say it, but Ben just moved to the top of our suspect list," Dom whispered as they slid into a small table on the outdoor dining deck of the *Gull View Inn* where they'd decided to grab a bite to eat while figuring out their next course of action.

Claire's lips thinned. "I can't imagine why he would disappear. It's not like him to run off and not tell Sarah. I wonder if Norma knows where he is. His disappearance may just be a manifestation of his grief for his mother."

"Or it could be that he *is* guilty, which would explain Norma's silence. She's been covering for him all along," Dom suggested.

"I'm sure that's not it," Claire said with an air of certainty that she didn't feel. The clues were stacking up oddly and covering for Ben did explain Norma's strange reluctance to tell them about her fight with Zoila. Norma would do anything for Ben—even go to jail. But what she couldn't figure was *why* Ben would kill Zoila. "Besides, I'm sure we can prove Ben couldn't have done it through his alibi at the hospice house."

"*If* he went there before he disappeared."

Claire tapped her foot under the table. Leave it to Dom to stick to the facts instead of taking the personalities into consideration. She was about to come out with a sarcastic reply when Velma showed up at her elbow, her blue eyes alive with excitement and an order pad and pencil in her hand.

"It's lovely to see you folks." She winked at them, then bent closer to the table, which didn't really bring her much closer considering her normal posture was at almost a ninety degree angle. She lowered her voice to just above a whisper. "How is the investigation going? Are you guys trying to clear Norma?"

Claire nodded. "Have you heard anything?"

Velma looked around to make sure no one was listening, then she shook her head. "I'm afraid not. Zambuco's in the dining room and he's pretty close-mouthed about the case."

Claire sighed. Had Zambuco coincidentally stopped in for lunch, or was Dom right in thinking the detective had been following them? Either way, the last thing she needed was Zambuco wandering over and interrupting them.

"Anyway, would you like to order?" Velma asked. "We're having a special on the haddock sandwiches today, but there's no Jonah crab soup because Ben didn't bring us any crabs today like he usually does."

Claire caught Dom's eye over their menus.

"Did you say Ben brings you live crabs?" Dom asked.

"Oh yes, every other day." Velma's snow-white bun bobbed up and down on her head as she nodded, then her face creased with concern. "But he hasn't been here in three days now."

"And he gets them from the island?" Dom persisted.

"Yes, there's only one spot you can get them here, you know."

"We know."

Velma stared at them expectantly and it took Claire a few minutes to realize she was waiting for their order. Claire's mind was too busy considering the ramifications of what she'd just heard.

"I'll take the house salad with oil and vinegar." Claire handed her menu over to Velma before she changed her mind and veered off track of her healthy eating regimen.

"And I'll have the meatball sandwich." Dom handed his menu over, too.

"Be back in a jiff." Velma turned on her heel and scurried off.

"This does not look good at all." Dom patted down his eyebrows while he stared out into the ocean.

"I know, but lots of people could go to that section of the island. The crab shells in the footprint don't mean much on their own ... Oh, that reminds me." Claire dug in her pocket for her cell phone. Lifting it up, she squinted at the display, wishing she'd brought her half-moon reading glasses. "These damn things are so hard to read in the light. Oh, there's three bars. Now let me send that text to Robby. We can't make any rash conclusions until we know the shoe size."

Claire sent the text, then looked back up to find Dom still staring out at the ocean. He was clearly deep in thought. Hopefully, not about how he was going to prove Ben was the killer.

"I think you are right," he said.

"Of course I am," Claire said. "About what?"

"The footprint. Something is wrong about it."

"That's what I thin—"

Claire was interrupted by the chirping of her phone. A text from Robby was on the screen. "The shoe size is twelve ... I don't know what size Ben takes. It was too smudged to see much of the tread. Oh, and he said the time of death was eight twenty-five."

Dom nodded, but kept silent while the waitress slid their plates onto the table. He lifted the top piece of bread to inspect the meatballs, then nodded his satisfaction when he saw they were lightly covered in sauce—just the way he liked them. "We need to find out who wears a size twelve shoe. The time of death can be very helpful."

Claire nodded as she worked on spearing a piece of lettuce, tomato and cucumber on her fork. She had it raised halfway to her lips when she sensed someone at her left elbow.

"So, you two are at it again." Zambuco stood next to the table, glaring down at them.

Claire gave him her most innocent look. "At what, Detective Zambuco?"

"You know what I'm talking about." Zambuco tapped his finger on the table. "You need to stop pestering Robby about things pertaining to the case ... like shoe sizes and time of death."

"Did you say time of death?"

Claire jumped at the voice coming from her right. Mae Biddeford sat one table over.

When had she come in?

Claire hadn't even noticed her. And now, here she was, her chair pushed back from her table and almost halfway to Claire and Dom's.

Claire glanced uneasily at Dom and Zambuco. She didn't really want the whole restaurant to be listening to the details of their investigation.

"I don't need you butting in, too. The case details are supposed to be kept inside the department." Zambuco gave Claire a pointed look and her heart pinched. She hoped she hadn't gotten Robby into trouble. She knew his confidence in doing his job as a cop was already pretty low and she didn't want to make him feel even worse.

"I'm not butting in," Mae said indignantly. "I might have information that is pertinent to the case. But if you're not interested ..."

Mae turned and scooted her chair a half-inch back toward her own table.

"What kind of information?" Zambuco bellowed.

Mae turned back around, then scooted her chair even closer than it was before. She was practically sitting at their table now. She tilted her head back and looked up at Zambuco, who towered over them.

"As you know, I bring a few jars of my jams over to the hospice house on Wednesdays as a donation." She paused, apparently waiting for them to make some sort of recognition of her generosity.

"That's so nice of you." Claire tried not to roll her eyes at Dom.

"Yes. Well, anyway, when I was signing in yesterday, I happened to notice that Norma had signed in before me. I always glance at the list ...

not that I'm nosy or anything, but one can hardly help looking at the other names when one signs in."

Dom leaned forward with interest. "And what time did she sign in?"

"Eight-fifteen," Mae said to Dom, then glanced back up at Zambuco. "So, you see, depending on the time of death, Norma might have a solid alibi."

Zambuco's eyes sparked with interest. "And she hadn't signed out?"

"No, she was still there. I peeked into Anna's room and saw her," Mae said. "The two of them had their heads bent together and were discussing something. It seemed important. Anna looked a little upset, so I didn't interrupt them."

Claire felt a ripple of hope. "So, Norma couldn't possibly have killed Zoila."

Mae's brows rose, and she brushed an imaginary piece of lint from her shoulder. "Well, I wouldn't know that, because I'm not privy to police information and I don't know the time of death."

"But if she had a solid alibi, why wouldn't she just tell the police?" Dom asked. "It would be so easy to verify."

Zambuco frowned down at Mae. "Are you sure about this? She didn't mention it."

"Sure as I'm sitting here. And there was another strange thing I noticed when I was there," Mae said eagerly.

"What's that? Another person on the list with an alibi?" Zambuco asked.

"Well, it wasn't so much anyone that was on the sign-in list, it was someone who was missing from the list."

"Missing? I don't understand."

"Well, there's someone who is always on there every Wednesday. Signs in two lines above me ... and yesterday, that name wasn't there."

"Well, who is it?" Claire asked impatiently, her stomach sinking as she feared she already knew the answer.

"Ben Campbell."

Chapter Nineteen

Claire flew down the steps of the *Gull View Inn* behind Zambuco.

"I hope you're not going to do what I think you're going to do," she yelled at his back.

"I thought you'd be happy. I'm going to let Norma Hopper out," he shouted over his shoulder.

"I am happy about that. But you can't be serious about suspecting Ben Campbell."

Zambuco whirled on her, causing her to pull up short. He scowled down at her, his gray eyebrows puckering over beady, black eyes. "Why not?"

"I just know he couldn't have done it."

"Listen. I know about your psych degree. I know you're well respected in the field, but I also know that you're friends with Ben. I think your friendship is clouding your judgment, and right now I need to follow the evidence."

Claire's brow furrowed. She wondered what, exactly, Zambuco had for evidence. "What evidence?"

Zambuco held up his large hand, ticking off the items on his cigar-like fingers. "Ben was seen riding away from Zoila's in an agitated state. Norma is covering for someone, and everyone knows Ben is like a son to her. The footprint near the body had Jonah crab shells and I just found out I can't get my favorite crab soup here because Ben hasn't delivered the crabs, so I know he frequents the spot that has those crabs. Ben was seen fleeing the zen garden the morning of Zoila's murder. Ben didn't show up at the hospice center to visit his mother that morning and, according to what a little birdie told me, no one has seen him since."

Claire's stomach sank. How did Zambuco know all that? Maybe he had been following them and questioning the same people, or maybe he was a competent detective in his own right. Either way, it didn't matter. He had a point. There was a lot of evidence against Ben.

"If that's not enough evidence to satisfy you, I don't know what to tell you." Zambuco turned and strode toward his car. "Now, if you'll excuse me, I have a new suspect to search for."

Claire slapped her arms against her sides in frustration as Zambuco slammed the car door and sped off. She felt someone beside her and turned to see Dom. "We can't let him arrest Ben."

"He probably won't be able to find him," Dom said wryly.

"What do we do now?"

"Well, if you're done with your lunch, I think we need to go find Ben and talk to him before Zambuco does. I'm not convinced he is the killer, either, and I'm not sure Zambuco will question him properly, given Ben's handicap."

Claire signed. "Great idea. You have any idea where we can find him?"

"No. But we should start where we always start. At his home."

"At Anna and Ben's place? I'm sure Sarah and Shane already looked there."

"Right, but with our trained eyes, we may be able to pick out a clue they missed."

Claire nodded. Dom was right. They had to start somewhere and it might as well be Ben's house.

***

Anna and Ben lived in a small, but meticulously cared for, home. Anna had updated the old cottage with vinyl shingles and new windows. Claire hadn't been there since Anna had been moved to the hospice facility on the mainland, but she was glad to see that Ben had kept it up. He'd even kept the plants in Anna's extensive garden trimmed.

Claire felt a pang of sadness as she looked over the garden. She'd heard from Norma that Ben probably wouldn't be able to keep up the payments on the house once Anna died and she hated to think of how losing the only home he'd ever known so soon after losing his mother would affect him.

Then again, if Zambuco had his way, Ben had bigger problems ahead of him. Claire brushed past the smooth winterberry holly plant and remembered how Porch Cat had brought a leaf to her patio.

Had the cat been trying to tell her something?

No, that was too crazy. She was starting to grasp at straws—best to stick to the clues at hand.

A trio of colorful pansies in clay pots stood on the front steps and Dom stuck his finger into one of the pots. "This dirt is moist. Someone has been here within the last thirty hours."

Claire nodded. She knew plants in pots dried out quickly and there had been no rain.

"Maybe Ben has been here the whole time. Hiding out in his house," she suggested.

"Why would he hide in the house if he wasn't guilty of something?"

Good question. Claire considered it, then thought of an answer. "Maybe something scared him enough to make him hide."

Dom rapped loudly on the door. "Ben! Are you in there? We just want to talk."

No answer.

Claire looked in the window beside the door. She couldn't detect any movement. "Ben, it's Claire. We can help you."

No answer.

"He may have been here earlier, but I don't think he's here now," Dom said as he peered in one of the windows. "It doesn't look like he left in a hurry. Everything is in its place."

Claire looked in beside him, craning her neck to see as far to each side as she could.

"Yeah, you'd think there would be some sort of mess if he left in a hurry. I wonder where he could be." Her heart clenched at the thought of Ben out there alone somewhere. The thought of him lonely and scared made her feel even worse as she looked at the pictures of a happy Ben, his shock of blond hair swooped over his forehead, the wide smile he always seemed to wear accentuating the dimple on his chin. "Look at how happy he is in the pictures. He was like that all the time, but now ..."

Dom squinted at the pictures and made a funny sound.

"What?" Claire asked.

Dom had that nagging feeling of something important in the back of his mind but he just couldn't pull it up. In his younger days, that never would have happened ... but now that he was near seventy, he found it happening more and more. "Oh, nothing. I just had a familiar feeling is all."

"You mean like deja vu?"

"Sort of, but it's not anything that will help us find a clue."

"That's too bad, because I feel like there has to be something here that will help us figure this whole thing out. We just need to take the time to find it."

"Too bad time just ran out." Dom nodded in the direction of the road and Claire turned, her stomach swooping as she saw the Mooseamuck Island police car pull in with Robby at the wheel and Zambuco riding shotgun. Zambuco folded himself out of the passenger seat and walked over to them.

"Well, fancy meeting you two here." Zambuco looked around the yard, then frowned down at Claire. "I thought I told you to stop butting in."

"We were just looking for Ben." Claire fisted her hands on her hips.

Robby shot her a warning glance over the hood of the car and Claire relaxed a little. No sense in getting into it with Zambuco. She knew by the look on Robby's face that she was pushing her luck.

"Did you find him?" Zambuco asked.

"No."

"Yeah. I doubt he's here." Zambuco walked over to the side of the house and looked into the back yard. "I have a warrant that gives me permission to search the premises. I'm going to start in the tool shed because breaking into the house is messy."

He jerked his head toward Robby and they all marched toward the back of the house. Robby and Zambuco snapped on white latex gloves. Claire felt her nerves prickling as they walked past Anna's prize rose bushes, then the empty space where she usually planted her vegetable garden and finally stopping at the shed with its row of tiger lilies lining the front, their tall stalks waiting for summer buds to bloom.

The shed door squealed as Robby slid it open and they all looked in. It was crammed full of gardening gear and various outdoor supplies. A snowblower sat in one corner, a giant wheelbarrow beside it.

"Let's go in, Skinner." Zambuco looked back over his shoulder at Claire and Dom. "You two stay out here. And don't touch anything."

Robby stepped in and Zambuco went in after him, tripping over the threshold and stepping on a shovel, then turning and stumbling over a pile of rakes that were leaning against the wall.

Dom watched him fumble with the rakes, amazed at how many kinds of rakes it takes to run a garden. There were old, rusty rakes, newer rakes with plastic tines, rakes with wooden handles, metal handles and even one with a fancy gold and maroon handle.

Zambuco reached in and pulled out one particular rake with a long, wooden handle and sharp metal tines at the end. He held up the tines and Dom's eyes widened as he noticed the rusty-colored stains on them—they were looking at Zoila's murder weapon.

Zambuco's face was grim as he came out of the shed, the rake held out away from his body in his glove-clad hand. "I guess we need to step up our search for Ben Campbell. He's no longer just a person of interest ... he's now a murder suspect."

Chapter Twenty

Zambuco left in a hurry, sending Claire and Dom on their way with a warning not to interfere in the search for Ben. Since neither of them had any idea where to start looking, they'd decided to split up and take a break until an idea presented itself.

Claire thought Norma might know where Ben was, but she was nowhere to be found, either.

Was Norma out looking for Ben?

Claire wanted to be looking, too, but it was late afternoon and her brain was getting foggy. The turn of events had stunned her and she needed a large cup of green tea to clear her thinking.

She stood at the sink overlooking her garden and the Atlantic Ocean beyond. The view from her spot on the hill was breathtaking, but Claire couldn't enjoy it. Ben's freedom was at stake and she just knew there was some other explanation for the rake being in his shed.

She set the teapot on the stove, grabbed some flax seed oil from the fridge, then took out a bottle of apple cider vinegar and two shot glasses from the cupboard. She poured apple cider vinegar into one glass and flax seed oil into the other.

Picking up the apple cider vinegar glass, she threw her head back and tossed the vile, caustic liquid down her throat. Coughing and sputtering, she reached for the flax seed oil to chase it with. It was noxious, but helped smooth out the acidity of the vinegar.

The healthy concoction left a nasty taste in her mouth, and Claire knew just what could fix it. Dark chocolate. Now, if she could just remember where she'd hidden it.

She rummaged through several drawers, her chest tightening as she came up empty. It was disturbing that she couldn't remember where she'd hidden them. Forty years ago, her mind was like a steel trap. Now? Not so much. Good thing she was diligent about her health regimen. She intended to remain healthy and active well into her nineties. Hopefully, that would help her mind stay healthy and active, too.

The tea kettle whistled and she reached into the cabinet where she kept the green tea, her spirits rising as her fingers curled around a thin square of dark chocolate.

"Aha! I remember now." She unwrapped the chocolate, popped it into her mouth, put a tea bag into her mug and then poured the boiling water over it.

Relishing the silky texture of the bittersweet chocolate melting in her mouth, Claire stepped out into her garden, her hand curled around the mug of steeping tea.

She walked down the garden path toward the edge of her property, as if drawn toward the sea. From the edge, she looked down at Crab Cove.

Was Zambuco down there talking to the fishermen?

She thought it was likely—he was probably trying to find out if Ben left the island after Zoila's murder.

Which made Claire wonder ... had Ben left the island, or was he safe somewhere? He would turn to either Sarah or Norma for help. Sarah denied knowing where Ben was and Claire believed her, which left Norma.

Norma had been in jail, but what if Ben had turned to her before she'd been jailed?

Claire wandered through her garden, pinching a dead bloom here and plucking a dead leaf there, her mind whirling with questions about the case.

Why hadn't Norma told the truth? She must have known she would have an alibi at the hospice house, but she'd let herself be jailed rather than tell anyone what her and Zoila had argued about or that she'd gone to visit Anna.

Did the murder have something to do with Anna?

If Ben wasn't the killer, then how did the murder weapon get in his shed?

Claire sipped her tea and looked out over the railing, feeling like a failure. She *used* to be able to solve these cases easily but she was much older now and out of practice. Still, this case was more important than any others because it involved her friends. Her fists tightened around the railing in frustration.

Down below, she could see Dom sitting on the bench that overlooked Long Sands Beach and wondered if he felt the same way she did. Were they too old to solve cases effectively?

Claire didn't think so. Her mind still worked pretty good. Even now, it was going over the facts and sifting through the different personalities, trying to find inconsistencies that could help her solve the case.

There was one discrepancy that niggled at her.

Why would Shane lie about the time he was at Zoila's the day before her murder?

Kenneth had said he'd seen Shane there at one o'clock, but Shane was pretty specific that he wasn't there until after three.

"Meow!"

Claire looked down to see Porch Cat weaving her way through the garden, her eyes slitted against the bright sunlight.

"Hi, kitty. I don't have anything for you today." Claire made a mental note to pick up some cat treats next time she was in town.

She watched the cat rub her face against the trellis where she was growing a border of Imposter roses. This was her first year trying the pink flowers that looked like a clematis, but were actually a rose that would bloom all summer long. Several buds had formed on the plant during the last week and Claire was anxious to see them bloom.

Porch Cat sniffed at the plant, then reached out a paw and touched one of the buds as if she was trying to figure out if it was a rose or a clematis.

"Fools you, doesn't it?" Claire sipped her tea and marveled at the plant. She never ceased to be amazed by nature, which fooled you into thinking things were one way when they were actually another.

She reached down to pet the cat, who was purring at her ankles. "In the garden, just like in life, things aren't always what they seem."

And then Claire realized what had been bothering her about Shane's lie. She ran into the house, tossed her mug into the sink, grabbed her car keys and rushed out the door.

She had to talk to Dom right away. They'd made a terrible mistake. They'd taken the evidence at face value and thought things were one way, when that really wasn't the case at all. And now, because of it, Zambuco was about to arrest the wrong person.

Chapter Twenty-One

Dom bit into the bocconotti cookie as he watched the waves lap at the beach. The confection, baked fresh this morning in the north end of Boston and delivered on the afternoon ferry, was lightly dusted in powdered sugar and bursting with strawberry jam. He barely tasted it, though. His mind was too busy trying to figure out where they'd gone wrong in solving the case.

Something didn't add up, but for the life of him, he couldn't figure out what it was. Maybe he really was losing his touch. He hadn't investigated a murder case in many years, and as much as he hated to admit it, he was getting older. But that was on the outside—on the inside, he still felt young and this case had rekindled his enthusiasm and made him feel alive for the first time since Sophia's death.

There were still so many unanswered questions.

Why would Shane lie about the time he was at Zoila's?

Who else was at the zen garden that morning? Was it the real killer who dropped the *Chowders* bag?

Why didn't Kenneth take the family pictures from Zoila's?

What was on that old paper Zoila was arguing with Norma over?

What was Norma hiding, or who was she protecting?

Was the sketch of Zoila's cabin a clue?

Dom was sure something happened the morning of Zoila's death that made it urgent for the killer to silence her, because otherwise it would have been much smarter to kill her in her remote cabin. The killer had taken a big chance doing it in the public garden.

Zoila had a paper in her hand when she'd argued with Norma that morning. It must have something to do with the paper, but what would be so important that someone would kill Zoila and Norma wouldn't say a thing about it?

And if Norma knew whatever it was that got Zoila killed, would the killer go after Norma next?

He pulled another cookie out of the bag as he continued to contemplate the case. He had to admit, the clues did seem to point to Ben.

Ben was seen rushing away from the murder scene on his bike.

The white bag from *Chowders* had been dropped in the area.

Ben had previously visited Zoila.

Norma had visited Ben's mother that morning and was now protecting someone with her silence.

Ben frequented the one spot on the island where you could find Jonah crab.

... And now Ben was missing.

But his instincts told him something about those clues were not as they seemed. Claire was adamant that Ben wasn't capable of murder and he trusted her judgment.

Dom watched a sandpiper scurrying along the water line, pecking at the sand on the very edge of the water, then scurrying back as each wave approached.

Dom watched as the bird darted forward, leaving little forked footprints in the sand, then scurried back, the wave erasing the footprints he'd just left.

Over and over, he darted forward along the shore and over and over, the waves drove him back and erased his footprints.

Dom admired his persistence ... and then Dom's eyebrows tingled electrically—he knew what had been bothering him all this time!

He jumped up from the bench. Shoving the bag of cookies in his pocket, he sprinted to his car for his cell phone. He had to contact Claire— they'd made a grave error in judgment and he hoped they could make up for it before it was too late!

***

Dom was almost to his car when Claire whipped into the parking lot, screeching to a stop beside him.

"I think I've figured part of it out—Shane wasn't the one who lied about what time he was at Zoila's, it was Kenneth!" Claire said excitedly. "I think he's trying to frame Ben."

Dom nodded. "Ben didn't do it and the footprint proves that."

"It does? But the footprint had the crab shells embedded in it."

"Precisely. Something's bothered me about that footprint all along and I just realized what it was. Zoila was killed violently, so there would have been a struggle, yet there was only one footprint there."

"So?"

"Don't you see, there would have been many footprints. The killer must have raked the sand to get rid of the footprints he made so they couldn't be used as evidence."

"And then Ben came along after and saw Zoila already dead! That's why he's disappeared ... he must have run off scared."

"We need to get in touch with Zambuco. Those crab shells in the footprint prove that Ben isn't the killer and I think the rake was planted in his shed. When Zambuco found the pile of rakes, I recognized one handle ... I didn't realize it at the time, but one of the handles matches the equipment I saw in Kenneth's barn."

"And if all that's true, my theory about Kenneth lying about the time they were at Zoila's instead of Shane being the one who lied makes sense. Kenneth knew Ben delivered lunches between noon and two, so he had to say he was there during that time frame in order to claim he'd seen Ben there. Ben never was at Zoila's that day."

"And Shane told the truth." Dom pressed his lips together, remembering the sand he'd felt under his feet at the counter that day. "The morning Zoila was killed, Kenneth came to the counter and then Shane came in after him. I felt sand under my feet when I went up and assumed it was from Shane ... but given what we know now, I think the sand might have been from Kenneth, who was standing there *before* Shane."

"So Kenneth killed Zoila?" Claire asked. "But why? And why frame Ben *and* how does Norma fit into this?"

Dom's face turned grim. "I couldn't figure that out, either, but I might have an idea as to why ... and if my theory is correct, Ben is in grave danger."

Chapter Twenty-Two

Claire desperately tried to get her cell phone to show some bars as they rushed to the point.

Where was Zambuco when they needed him?

Unfortunately, the detective was no longer following them around town. Dom and Claire were on their own.

To make matters worse, a thunderstorm was rolling in. Dark, gray clouds hung over the ocean adding a menacing feel, and the air felt alive with humid electricity. It was early dusk, but the clouds had made it darker than normal. Naturally, the lights were off in the Bennett mansion and just when Claire thought the scene couldn't get any more cliche, the sky lit up and a boom of thunder split the air just as they skidded to a stop in the circular driveway.

Fat drops of rain splattered on the car as they jumped out.

"The barn." Dom pointed toward the barn where a slice of yellow light spilled out from underneath the door and they made their way over quietly.

Claire's heart pounded as they stopped outside the door. Dom put his finger up to his lips to indicate silence and Claire rolled her eyes. After a career of consulting with the police, she knew enough to be quiet.

Voices wafted out from inside and she leaned forward to hear what they were saying while the rain drops soaked her hair and ran down her neck.

"Just write it on the paper and I won't hurt you." Claire cringed at the menacing tone in Kenneth's voice.

"But I didn't kill her." Ben's voice, trusting and innocent. Claire glanced at Dom, who was preening his eyebrows as he edged his way around the door trying to get inside.

Claire felt anger flood her chest. Kenneth was trying to frame Ben for Zoila's murder. He'd make a good scapegoat, too—his simple nature allowed him to be easily manipulated and he wasn't equipped to defend himself.

But she still couldn't figure out one thing ... why had Kenneth killed Zoila in the first place?

"Kenny, I'm hungry." The pleading tone in Ben's voice speared Claire's heart and she bit her lip to keep quiet. She shuffled to the right, hiding behind a stack of boxes just inside the door so she could get a better look at what was going on.

Ben sat in the middle of the barn, his legs and torso tied to a metal chair. He had a pen and a piece of paper in his hand. Kenneth loomed over him, his back to Claire.

"Listen, you little jerk, just write the letter and I'll get you a pizza."

"But I didn't do it. I can't lie!"

Kenneth kicked the chair.

Ben cried out.

The lights flickered.

A deafening clap of thunder caused Claire to jump, dislodging the boxes which clattered to the floor.

Kenneth whirled around in her direction.

Claire's heart froze. She was caught.

Claire was unable to move. She realized she'd made a big mistake. She didn't have the power of an armed police team behind her like in the old days. All she had was Dom ... and he didn't even have a gun.

Too bad Kenneth *did* have one, and he was pointing it at her right now.

"You!" Kenneth sneered. "I should have taken care of you when you were here before. But I'll just have to get rid of you now. Looks like Ben might have to kill you, too."

Claire's heart started up again. Kenneth was focusing on her, which meant he hadn't spotted Dom.

Was Dom still hidden outside the door?

She didn't dare look in that direction, afraid Kenneth might catch on that someone else was there if she did. Without a gun, she didn't know how helpful Dom would be, but at least he could run for the car and drive to the police.

"What are you talking about, Kenny? I didn't kill Claire—she's right here." Ben turned trusting eyes on Claire and her heart pinched.

Kenneth snorted. "I might have to change your note. You killed Zoila and Claire found out and confronted you, then you had to kill her, too. The guilt was too much so you killed yourself."

"No." Ben shook his head. "I did not hurt Zoila. I saw her lying in the garden."

"It's okay, Ben," Claire soothed, partly because her heart ached for Ben and partly because she knew her best chance of escape was to keep Kenneth talking while Dom ran for help. "We know you didn't hurt Zoila. Kenneth did."

Ben scrunched up his face and turned to Kenneth. "Why?"

"Yeah. Why *did* you kill Zoila?" Claire echoed.

"You and your great detective friend, Benedetti, couldn't figure it out?"

Claire crossed her arms over her chest. "Well, we figured out it was you ..."

"Yeah. You see, I had to stop her. I couldn't give half my fortune to him." Kenneth jerked his head toward Ben.

"Half your fortune? What are you—?" Claire looked from Kenneth to Ben and then to Kenneth again. Her mouth dropped open when realization dawned on her.

She remembered Dom's feeling of deja-vu when they were at Ben's house, and now she knew what it was even if Dom hadn't recognized it himself. Ben and Kenneth bore an uncanny resemblance to each other, right down to the cleft chin which Claire knew was a genetic trait ... one that Silas Barrett also had.

Kenneth and Ben were half-brothers.

Chapter Twenty-Three

"Zoila found out you were brothers," Claire said softly.

Kenneth looked at Ben with contempt. "*Half*-brothers. Dear old Daddy couldn't be faithful."

"And Zoila was going to tell."

"That's right," Kenneth said. "Like most of the sappy islanders here, she had a soft spot for Ben and thought he should get a cut of the Barrett fortune. She had proof in Daddy's own hand that he wanted it that way, and she said she'd give me one day to tell Ben myself and or she was going to tell him. She had a meeting with Ben that morning at the zen garden, but I got there first."

"That's the paper that she and Norma were arguing about," Claire said.

"Norma?"

"Yes, they argued right before she died. That's why Zambuco arrested her."

"Arrested her?" Kenneth's face crumbled. "But that means that Norma knows..."

"That's right." Claire saw her chance and decided to take advantage of her psych skills to try to persuade Kenneth into giving up. "Norma knows and Dom knows, too, so it won't do you any good to kill me and Ben. It's better to give yourself up now and I'll help persuade the judge to go lenient on you."

Another clap of thunder, and Claire almost peed her pants as she watched Kenneth's gun wave around in his hand. His eyes had taken on a glazed look and were darting from her to Ben.

"I won't give up! No one will believe Norma, she's too crotchety. And I'll have to make sure that old washed up detective, Benedetti, meets with an accident."

Kenneth advanced toward Claire and brought his gun level with her forehead. She heard the click of the safety and she felt like a stone was lodged in her throat as she wracked her brain for something to say to persuade him to give her the gun.

She opened her mouth to speak but was silenced by another clap of thunder. The sound of a gunshot rang in her ears.

And then the lights went out.

***

Dom burst through the door just as the lights went out. He didn't know if Claire had been hit or not, but his old cop instincts kicked in and he launched himself in the direction of Kenneth without even thinking twice. As he flew through the air toward the gunman, he vaguely remembered that he didn't have a Kevlar vest on, but he wasn't concerned with his own safety. There were two people in danger in there and he had to do what he could to keep them safe.

The lights flickered on again just as Dom crashed into Kenneth, sending them both to the floor amidst the sharp report of another gunshot.

Out of the corner of his eye, he saw Claire rushing toward them. She kicked out at Kenneth, trying to dislodge the gun but to no avail.

"Let go, old man!" Kenneth yelled as he brought his knee up hard into Dom's stomach.

Dom grunted in pain, but managed to keep his grip on the hand with the gun. Claire kicked out again, this time connecting with Dom in a fatal mistake that caused him to loosen his hold.

Kenneth rolled away and sprang to his feet, waving his gun between Claire and Dom.

"Killing you two is going to be fun." Kenneth jerked the gun toward the middle of the barn where Ben was tied up. "Get over by Ben. That way, I can take care of the three of—"

"*Meow!*" A bundle of black and brown fur came flying down from the loft, landing on Kenneth's arm with all claws extended. Kenneth waved his hand to dislodge the cat, losing his grip on the gun that landed in the corner with a clatter.

Claire ran for the gun.

Dom ran for Kenneth, plowing into him like a linebacker. They rolled around on the floor again. This time, Dom had the advantage over Kenneth, whose cat-scratched arm slowed him down.

Dom managed to get Kenneth over onto his stomach and, with his knee on his back, he jerked his arms behind him.

Claire rushed over, the gun safe in her hand.

"Ben, are you okay?" Claire asked. Dom managed to look over to see Ben smiling down at Porch Cat, who was curled in his lap licking her paws leisurely. Before Dom turned away, the cat turned her bright green eyes on him and he could have sworn she winked.

Dom shoved his knee harder into Kenneth's back.

"Not so bad for an old washed up detective, eh?" Dom's chest swelled with pride. He wasn't too old to chase bad guys after all.

Kenneth didn't have time to answer because just then, the barn door burst open and a voice yelled:

"Hands up in the air and don't move!"

***

194

"Robby, what are you doing here?" Claire was surprised to see her nephew standing alone in the doorway. Surprised that he'd known they were there *and* that he'd had the guts to bust in on his own after hearing the shots. She knew he'd never been in a situation this dangerous before and the look on his face alternated between pride and terror as he took in the situation.

"What's going on here?" Robby asked, his eyes darting from Claire to Ben to Kenneth and Dom on the ground.

"Kenneth kidnapped Ben ... he was the killer all along," Claire blurted out.

Robby's eyes widened. "He killed Zoila? But why?"

Claire explained how Zoila had discovered the relation between Kenneth and Ben and was going to tell everyone. "Apparently, Kenneth didn't want Ben to get any of the Barrett money."

Robby scowled down at Kenneth. "I never did like him. Is everyone okay?"

"I could use a little help with the bad guy," Dom said from his position on the floor, where he was still holding Kenneth down.

"Right. Of course." Robby hurriedly holstered his gun and took a set of handcuffs off his belt, then knelt down and snapped them on Kenneth's wrists. Dom stood up and Claire noticed his leg was oozing with sticky, red blood.

"You've been shot!" Claire pointed to Dom's leg and they all turned to look.

Dom looked down, then back up at them, a sheepish grin spreading on his face.

"That's not blood," He pulled out a bakery bag from of his pocket—the outside was stained with red goo. "It's my bocconottis. They must have gotten squished in the scuffle."

"Can you guys untie me?" Ben asked in a small voice, and Claire ran over and started loosening the ropes while Robby pulled the now docile Kenneth to his feet.

"Kenny did something bad? Are you arresting him?" Ben stood up shakily and lowered Porch Cat gently to the floor. The cat strolled over to Dom and licked a blob of jelly that was on his pants, then turned her back to him and strolled off.

"I'm afraid so," Claire said, then turned to Robby. "How did you know we were in here?"

"I knew Ben wasn't a murderer and I figured you two knew more about what was really going on than anyone else, so I took a play out of Zambuco's book and followed you."

"Well, you got here just in time." Dom glanced over at Claire. "I don't know if we could have pulled off the capture if it wasn't for you."

Robby's face turned red. "Well, it looked like you had things pretty much tied up when I got here. I didn't do much."

"Oh, that's not true," Dom said graciously. "You played a critical role. Isn't that right, Claire?"

"Yep, we were struggling ... you came in just at the right time," Claire said earnestly.

"Well ... if you guys say so." Robby straightened with obvious pride and Claire shot Dom a grateful look. Capturing Kenny would do wonders for Robby's self-esteem and who knew, maybe he'd even share clues in the future without her having to bribe him with baked goods.

"I gotta secure the prisoner in my police car and call this in." Robby nodded at them and propelled Kenneth out the door.

Ben followed quickly behind them, asking Robby if he could ride in the police car, too.

Claire and Dom trailed at a more leisurely pace. Claire noticed the rain had stopped as they stepped outside. Thunder roiled in the distance but softer now, not the loud claps they'd heard when the storm was overhead. Robby already had Kenneth in the back of the car and could be heard on the police radio.

"That's right, you can call off the search for Ben Campbell—I have him with me. But he's not the murderer. Kenneth Barrett is and I've captured him, too."

Claire heard something crackle across the radio, then Robby's voice again:

"By myself. Well, almost ... I had two civilians help ... Yes, *those* two civilians ..."

Claire and Dom exchanged raised-brow looks. Robby must have been talking to Zambuco, and Claire figured he'd guess it was her and Dom. They walked past Robby toward her car.

"We don't need to take the credit for this one, right?" Claire asked.

"Of course not. We've had plenty of credit in our day. Now, we do it just for fun." Dom reached into the bakery bag and pulled out a smooshed cookie. "You want a bocconotti?"

The squished thing oozing red goo in Dom's hand looked more like some sort of amputated body part than a cookie. Claire didn't find it the least bit appetizing—and anyway, sugar wasn't part of her health regimen.

"No, thanks." Claire glanced back at the barn. "I'm glad you busted in like that and saved us, but that was dangerous. Why didn't you just take off in the car and go to the police station."

Dom's face was thoughtful as he chewed his cookie. He swallowed, then shrugged. "I never even considered driving away in the car. I guess my police training kicked in. This old dog still has some tricks in him."

Claire smiled. She was glad to see *she* still had some tricks in her, too. "We did pretty good working together."

Dom nodded and held his knuckles out for a fist tap. "It feels good to be useful even if we are a bit rusty."

"Yeah, I'm glad we still have our skills. Too bad we won't get a chance to use them again any time soon."

Dom's face fell with disappointment. "Why not?"

"Until this week, there hadn't been a murder on Mooseamuck Island in over a hundred years. What are the odds another one will happen any time soon?"

Dom glanced up at the clearing sky, then smoothed his bushy eyebrows. He thought for a few seconds, then looked back at Claire with twinkling eyes.

"It's hard to say, but with no murders in the past hundred years, perhaps Mooseamuck Island is due for a few more."

Chapter Twenty-Four

"And Dom burst in and saved everyone?" Mae asked, looking at Dom with a level of admiration that made him extremely uncomfortable.

"Oh, no, I just tried to subdue Kenneth until Robby got there. Robby's the one who saved us," Dom replied graciously. He was happy to give Robby the credit and fend off Mae's unwanted attention, especially since he noticed Tom Landry frowning at the way Mae was looking at him.

"Well, I didn't really do anything ..." Robby stammered.

"Oh, yes, you did," Claire cut in. "You figured out who the real killer was and that something was going on at the point. Why, if you hadn't come in when you did, there's no telling what might have happened."

"What about Zambuco?" Jane craned her neck, looking around the diner. "Did he just take off into the wild blue yonder?"

Robby nodded. "He took Kenneth back to the jail on the mainland."

"Well, you showed him us islanders don't need any help from the mainland police," Tom said.

"I don't know about that." Robby lowered his voice. "He did put me in for a commendation, but I don't think we've seen the last of him."

Robby blushed as Sarah put a mug of coffee down in front of him. "That's on the house, Officer Skinner."

Sarah shot Claire and Dom a knowing look as she walked away. They'd never figured out what her secret was, but had promised they wouldn't let on they knew she had one. Claire thought that was just as well. It had nothing to do with Zoila's murder and Sarah deserved her privacy.

Besides, she'd probably come to Moosamuck Island to get away from whatever it was that was such a secret, and it was no one's business but Sarah's. Claire watched Sarah and Shane exchange special smiles as Sarah made her way back behind the counter and her heart lifted. She hoped whatever had plagued Sarah in her previous life was well behind her now.

"I still don't understand why you didn't say something, Norma." Jane turned to Norma, who sat at the end of the table, her floppy hat casting a shadow onto her plate of Maine blueberry pancakes

"Well, you wouldn't," Norma said gruffly. "You young people don't understand things like loyalty. I gave Anna my word all those years ago, and I ain't be going breaking it now."

"Even though you ended up in jail?" Lucy asked.

Norma snorted. "Jail doesn't scare me. The food's actually pretty good, you know. But if I'd known Kenneth would kidnap Ben, I might have said something. When I got out of jail, I knew Ben was missing and I looked everywhere for him. I just thought he was hiding. It never occurred to me Kenneth might try to kill him."

"So Anna never wanted Ben to get any money from Silas?" Mae asked. "Seems like she would have wanted that for him. I mean, the Barrett's have a bundle."

Norma's eyes took on a faraway look. "Anna's judgment was clouded when it came to Silas Barrett. He was a good guy when we were young. He and Anna were head over heels. But when his father died and he took over the Bennett family fortune, he changed into a hard, angry man. He would hardly give us the time of day, anymore. I guess he thought we were beneath him.

"Anna had one indiscretion with him after that and the result was Ben. But she never told Silas Ben was his son. I'm not sure how Silas found out, but Anna didn't want anything to do with him and she didn't want Ben soiled by his money. She was afraid Ben would end up a spoiled brat, like Kenneth."

"Will Ben get all of it now?" Mae asked.

"With Kenneth in jail, he'll be in charge of the estate. I hired some smarty pants financial folks from the mainland to help him," Norma said. "At least he won't hurt for money, which should actually give Anna some comfort. And being the same sweet old Ben, he's putting a lot of money into Kenneth's defense. He said that Kenneth is his family now and family does what it can to help out family."

"So it looks like Anna's worries over money changing Ben were for nothing." Claire sipped her red rooibos tea. "I just hope Kenneth appreciates what Ben is doing and treats him like a real brother."

"Just how did you figure out they *were* brothers?" Tom asked.

"It took a while for my old noggin to process the clues," Dom said. "But then they all came together. In the end, it was really one thing that stood out. Zoila had called Kenneth out to the cabin to give him some old family photos and paintings she'd discovered in the cabin. But Kenneth didn't take them. When Claire and I went out to investigate the cabin, we found them in the shed. The paper backing of one of them was split and it didn't dawn on me until later that people used to hide important documents behind pictures like that. I guess Silas must have had something documenting Ben's parentage and Zoila stumbled across it when she was handling the picture."

"That's right," Norma mumbled around a mouthful of pancake. "I guess old Silas had some sort of proof and a codicil to his will. I'm not sure why he had it hidden in the picture, but my guess is he was waiting for the right time to drop the bomb on Kenneth. Or maybe he wasn't even sure *if* he wanted to make it public at all. If you remember, he died suddenly and I guess he never got a chance to show it to anyone."

"And Zoila thought it should be made public ... or was she blackmailing Kenneth?" Mae asked slyly.

"Oh, no. She thought Ben should get his share. In fact, she tried to get me to help her persuade Kenneth to tell Ben himself." Norma looked at Claire. "That's what you saw us arguing about that morning."

"In the jail when you were sketching Zoilas cabin, were you trying to give us a clue?" Dom asked.

"Maybe." Norma looked at Dom with a twinkle in her eye. "I figured you'd be too dense to catch on, though."

"But we *did* catch on. Sort of. We did go to the cabin, which led to Dom figuring it out," Claire said. "Well that and a few other clues."

"Oh, what were they?" Jane asked.

"One thing that really stuck with me was that we thought Shane had lied about the time he visited Zoila the day before the murder. We couldn't figure out why," Claire replied. "And then we realized that wasn't the case at all. It was *Kenneth* who had lied."

Jane's brow creased. "Why would he do that?"

"He wanted to place Ben at Zoila's that day so we'd think they had some kind of argument. He knew Ben only delivered food between noon and two, so he had to lie and say he was there during that time."

"He sure did a lot of planning to frame Ben," Tom said.

"He did," Dom agreed. "He planted the murder weapon in Ben's shed, too. Except he made another mistake there. He'd taken the zen garden rake home and hidden it among the tools in his barn right after he killed Zoila. He figured no one would notice it there and he could keep it until an opportune moment presented itself to plant it at Ben's place. Except when the time came, he didn't know which one was the rake from the zen garden. So he took all the rakes to

Ben's. Claire and I were there when Zambuco pulled the murder weapon from Ben's shed. I saw the rake with the Bennett family colors in the pile and I knew something was off, but not exactly what that *something* was."

"But he wasn't going to just frame Ben for the murder," Claire added. "He was going to have Ben write up a fake confession saying he killed Zoila because she 'saw' something he didn't like in her vision, and then he planned to kill him and make it look like Ben had killed himself because he couldn't live with the guilt."

"That would solve both his problems. No one would be around to tell that Ben was Silas's son and even if someone did find out years later, Ben wouldn't be around to stake a claim on any of the Barrett money," Jane said.

"Yep. Kenneth had already burned the paper that Zoila found."

"But didn't Kenneth realize that Norma would have told the truth if anything happened to Ben?" Tom asked.

"He actually didn't know that Norma knew about it," Dom replied. "He was too busy implementing his plan and abducting Ben to pay attention to what was going on in town, so he had no idea Norma and Zoila had argued or even that Norma had been arrested."

"That's right,' Claire chimed in. "Zoila had asked Ben to meet her at the zen garden that morning. She'd already given Kenneth the ultimatum to tell Ben himself. She made the mistake of telling Kenneth where and when she was meeting Ben, and Kenneth got there first and killed her. Ben came along after and found her dead. He left his footprint in the sand and dropped the take-out bag from *Chowders* that Banes found in the woods as he ran away. He said he'd been taking a donut to Zoila."

"Meanwhile, Kenneth came into the diner to gather information," Dom continued. "Then he waited until he knew Ben was at home alone, brought the rake over and kidnapped Ben."

"Well, you guys certainly are brave, risking a run-in with a killer,' Mae twittered.

Dom waved his hand dismissively. "We have special training."

Claire pushed up from the table as the others kept talking. She needed some quiet time and there was a bench outside the restaurant that overlooked the cove, which was the perfect place for quiet reflection.

She curled her hand around her tea mug and sat on the bench, watching the boats sway on their moorings and listening to the seagulls' call. The smell of salt air and fried food made her lips curl in a smile. Investigating the murder had been fun, but she was glad things had quieted down.

"*Meow.*"

Claire looked down to see Porch Cat meandering through the colorful impatiens that were planted alongside the front of the restaurant.

"Hey, kitty." Claire held out her hand and the cat came over. Claire noticed she was carrying something in her mouth.

"What do you have there?"

Porch Cat sat in front of Claire and gazed up at her. Claire noticed that in the sunlight, the cat's green eyes were loaded with gold flecks which sparkled in the sunlight.

Porch Cat flicked her tail, then bent over and spit something out on the ground.

Claire looked down to see that it was a plump, juicy blackberry, which was odd since blackberries didn't come into season for another month. She remembered how Porch Cat had spit out the smooth winterberry holly leaf from Anna's rare plant on her patio and wondered if the cat had been trying to tell her something.

Maybe she'd been trying to lead her to Anna's. And if so, was this blackberry a clue? But a clue to what? Zoila's murder had already been solved.

Claire felt a mixture of trepidation and excitement as she remembered Dom's words about Mooseamuck Island being 'due' for a few more murders. Maybe the cat was trying to tell her another murder lay just around the corner.

That's silly, Claire thought as she watched the cat disappear under the leaves of a lush rhododendron. Porch Cat was just your average Maine Coon ... she didn't have any powers of premonition and stray cats didn't go around dropping clues at your feet.

Claire settled back on the bench and took another sip of tea as she eyed the empty space where Porch Cat had been a few seconds ago. Zoila's murder investigation had taken a lot of energy and she needed to rest up and replenish her strength.

She made a mental note to beef up her health regimen. She wanted to be sure she was in top condition with lots of energy to spare ... just in case another murder investigation happened to come her way.

The end.

A Note From The Author

Thanks so much for reading, *"A Zen For Murder"*. I hope you liked reading it as much as I loved writing it. If you did, and feel inclined to leave a review, I really would appreciate it.

This is book one of the Mooseamuck Island Cozy Mystery series. I plan to write many more books with Dom and Claire. I have several other series that I write, too - you can find out more about them on my website http://www.leighanndobbs.com.

Also, if you like this book, you might like my Mystic Notch series which is set in the White Mountains of New Hampshire and filled with magic and cats. I have an excerpt from the first book "Ghostly Paws" at the end of this book.

This book has been through many edits with several people and even some software programs, but since nothing is infallible (even the software programs), you might catch a spelling error or mistake and, if you do, I sure would appreciate it if you let me know - you can contact me at: lee@leighanndobbs.com.

Oh, and I love to connect with my readers, so please do visit me on facebook at http://www.facebook.com/leighanndobbsbooks

Signup to get my newsletter and take advantage of my early buyer discount:
http://www.leighanndobbs.com/newsletter

If you want to get a text message on your cell phone when I have a new release text COZYMYSTERY to 88202 (sorry, this only works for US cell phones!)

About The Author

Leighann Dobbs has had a passion for reading since she was old enough to hold a book, but she didn't put pen to paper until much later in life. After a twenty-year career as a software engineer with a few side trips into selling antiques and making jewelry, she realized you can't make a living reading books, so she tried her hand at writing them and discovered she had a passion for that, too! She lives in New Hampshire with her husband, Bruce, their trusty Chihuahua mix, Mojo, and beautiful rescue cat, Kitty.

Find out about her latest books and how to get discounts on them by signing up at:

http://www.leighanndobbs.com/newsletter
Connect with Leighann on Facebook
http://facebook.com/leighanndobbsbooks

More Books By Leighann Dobbs:

Mystic Notch
Cats & Magic Cozy Mystery Series
* * *

Ghostly Paws
A Spirited Tail

Blackmoore Sisters
Cozy Mystery Series
* * *

Dead Wrong
Dead & Buried
Dead Tide
Buried Secrets
Deadly Intentions

Lexy Baker
Cozy Mystery Series
* * *

Lexy Baker Cozy Mystery Series Boxed Set Vol 1
(Books 1-4)

Or buy the books separately:

Killer Cupcakes (Book 1)
Dying For Danish (Book 2)

Murder, Money and Marzipan (Book 3)
3 Bodies and a Biscotti (Book 4)
Brownies, Bodies & Bad Guys (Book 5)
Bake, Battle & Roll (Book 6)
Wedded Blintz (Book 7)
Scones, Skulls & Scams (Book 8)
Ice Cream Murder (Book 9)
Mummified Meringues (Book 10)

Kate Diamond
Adventure/Suspense Series
* * *

Hidden Agemda

Contemporary
Romance
* * *

Sweet Escapes
Reluctant Romance

Dobbs "Fancytales"
Regency Romance Fairytales Series
* * *

Something In Red

Snow White and the Seven Rogues
Dancing On Glass
The Beast of Edenmaine
The Reluctant Princess

Excerpt From Ghostly Paws

In over thirty years as head librarian for the Mystic Notch Library, Lavinia Babbage had never once opened the doors before eight a.m.

I knew this because my bookstore sat across the street and three doors down from the library. Every day, I passed its darkened windows on my way to work. I watched Lavinia turn on the lights and open the doors every single morning at precisely eight a.m. from inside my shop.

Most days I didn't pay much attention to the library, though. It was really the last thing on my mind as I walked past, my mind set on sorting through a large box of books I'd purchased at an estate sale earlier in the week. The edges of my lips curled in a smile as I thought about the gold placard I'd had installed on the oak door of the old bookshop just the day before. *Wilhelmina Chance, Proprietor.* That made things official— the shop was mine and I was back in my hometown, Mystic Notch, to stay.

I hurried down the street, deep in my own thoughts. The early morning mist, which wrapped itself around our sleepy town in the White Mountains of New Hampshire, had caused the pain to flare in my leg, and I forced myself not to limp. I continued along, my head down and engrossed in my thoughts when I nearly tripped over something gray and furry. My cat, Pandora, had stopped short in front of me causing me to do a painful sidestep to avoid squashing her.

"Hey, what the heck?"

Pandora blinked her golden-green eyes at me and jerked her head toward the library ... or at least it seemed like she did. Cats didn't actually jerk their heads toward things, though, did they?

Of course they didn't.

I looked in the direction of the library anyway. That's when I noticed the beam of light spilling onto the granite steps from the half-open library door.

Which was odd, since it was only ten past seven.

My stomach started to feel queasy. Lavinia never opened up this early. Should I venture in to check it out? Maybe Lavinia had come in early to catch up on restocking the bookshelves before the library opened. But she never left the door open like that. She was as strict as a nun about keeping that door closed.

I stood on the sidewalk, staring at the medieval-looking stone library building, my pre-caffeine fog making it difficult for me to decide what to do.

Pandora had no such trouble deciding. She raced up the steps past me. With a flick of her gray tail, she darted toward the massive oak door, shooting a reproachful look at me over her shoulder before disappearing into the building.

I took a deep breath and followed her inside.

"Lavinia? You in here?" My words echoed inside the library as I pushed the heavy oak door open, its hinges groaning eerily. The library was as still as a morgue with only the sound of the grandfather clock marking time in the corner broke the silence.

"Lavinia? You okay?"

No one answered.

I crept past the old oak desk, stacked with books ready to return to the library shelves. The bronze bust of Franklin Pierce, fourteenth president of the United States, glared at me from the end of the hall. I didn't have a good feeling about this.

"Meow." The sound came from the back corner where the stone steps lead to the lower level. Dammit! I'd warned Lavinia about those steps. They were steep and she wasn't that steady on her feet anymore.

I headed toward the back, my heart sinking as I noticed Lavinia's cane lying at the top of the stairs.

"Lavinia?" Rounding the corner, my stomach dropped when I saw a crumpled heap at the bottom of the stairs ... Lavinia.

I raced down the steps two at a time, my heart pounding as I took in the scene. Blood on the steps. Lavinia laying there, blood in her gray hair. She'd fallen and taken it hard on the way down. But she could still be alive.

I bent down beside her, taking her wrist between my fingers and checking for a pulse.

Lavinia's head tilted at a strange angle. Her glassy eyes stared toward the room where she kept new book arrivals before cataloguing them. I dropped her wrist, ending my search for a pulse.

Lavinia Babbage had stamped her last library book.

***

I called my sister Augusta, or Gus as I called her, who also happened to be the sheriff, and sat on the steps to wait. I might have drifted off, still sleepy from the lack of caffeine, because the next thing I heard was Augusta's voice in my ear.

"Willa, are you okay?"

I opened one eye to the welcome sight of the steaming Styrofoam coffee cup that Gus was holding out to me.

"I'm fine," I said, reaching for the cup.

"What happened?" I studied Gus who stood on the steps in front of me. No one would have guessed we were sisters. She was petite, her long, straight blonde hair tied back in a ponytail, which, I assume, she thought made her look more sheriff-like. Even in the un-flattering sheriff's uniform, you could tell she had an almost perfect hourglass figure. I was tall with thick wavy red hair, my figure more rounded—voluptuous, as some described me. The only thing we had in common was our amber colored eyes—same as our mom's.

"I was on my way to open the bookstore when I noticed the lights on in the library." I glanced down the street toward the municipal parking lot.

Now that the spring warm-up was here, I was trying to work in some extra exercise by parking in the lot two blocks away instead of on the street near the bookstore.

"Was that unusual?" Gus asked.

"Yep." I looked over my shoulder at the front door of the library. "It sure was. Lavinia never opens the library before eight. Plus the front door was cracked open, and she never leaves it open."

Gus started up the steps toward the library. "Did you touch anything?"

I stood up, wincing at the pain in my left leg—a reminder of the near fatal accident over a year ago that was one of the catalysts for my move back to Mystic Notch. The accident had left me with a slight limp, a bunch of scars and a few odd side effects I didn't like to dwell on.

"Nope, other than Lavinia. I didn't know if she was alive and needed aid," I said as I followed Gus into the library.

Gus stopped just inside the door and looked around. The coppery smell of blood tinged the air, making me lose interest in my coffee.

"It doesn't seem like anything is out of place ... no sign of struggle," she said.

"Nope, I think she just fell down the stairs." I started toward the back. "You know she was getting on in years and not that steady on her feet."

We turned the corner and my stomach clenched at the sight of Lavinia at the bottom of the steps.

"That's her cane?" Gus pointed to the purple metal cane, which was still lying as I'd found it.

"Yep. Looks like she lost her balance, dropped the cane, and fell."

Gus descended the stairs, her eyes carefully taking in every detail. She knelt beside Lavinia, studying her head. "She's pretty banged up."

"I know. These stairs are hard stone. I guess they can do a number on you." I winced as I looked at the bloody edges of the steps.

"So, you think this was an accident?"

"Sure. I mean, what else could have happened?"

"Yeah, you're probably right. No reason to suspect foul play." Gus stood and looked back up the stairs, down the hall and then back at Lavinia.

Her lips were pressed in a thin line and I wondered what she was thinking. I knew she was a good cop, but the truth was I didn't really know her all that well. Eight years separated us and she was just a teenager when I'd moved down south. Now, twenty-five years later, we were just becoming acquainted as adults.

"Mew." Pandora sat on the empty table in the storage room where Lavinia temporarily stored new books or returns before she catalogued them. I'd forgotten she was here. She wasn't really my cat ... well, not until recently. I'd inherited her along with the bookstore and my grandmother's house. I still wasn't used to being followed around by a feline.

"Isn't that Pandora?" Gus asked. Gus had been close to grandma—closer than I had, and it was somewhat of a mystery that Grandma had left me the shop, her house and the cat. In her will, she'd said she'd wanted me to come back home and have a house and business, which was odd because the timing had been perfect. She'd left a tidy sum of money for Gus, so at least there were no hard feelings.

"Yeah, she rides to work with me."

Gus raised a brow at me, but didn't say anything. Pandora stared at us—her intelligent, greenish-gold eyes contrasting eerily with her sleek gray fur.

"So, if it was unusual for Lavinia to be here at this time of the morning, why do you think she was here and what do you think she was doing?" Gus asked.

"I'm not sure."

Gus reached out to pet Pandora, who still sat on the table staring at us. "Are there any mice in here, Pandora? Maybe Lavinia heard something down here and wanted to investigate."

"Maybe." I looked around the floor for evidence of mice. Lavinia ran a pretty tight ship so I doubted there would be any mice in the library. And, since the room was empty of books, she hadn't come in early to catalogue new arrivals.

Which begged the question ... why *was* Lavinia in the library this early in the first place?

Made in the USA
Middletown, DE
20 June 2020